ALSO BY AR

A Summer Soundtrack
The Faerie Hounds of York
The Bayou

THE FLOS MAGICAE SERIES

<u>A Novel</u>
A Novel Arrangement

<u>Supplemental Novellas</u>
The Botanist's Apprentice
Winter's Dawn
The Solstice Cabin

THE BACHELOR'S VALET

◆ ◆ ◆

Flos Magicae

ARDEN POWELL

The Bachelor's Valet
Copyright © 2021 by Arden Powell

This is a work of fiction. Names, characters, places, and incidents either are the product of the author's imagination or are used fictitiously. Any resemblance to actual persons, living or dead, events, or locales is entirely coincidental.

Cover art and book design by Arden Powell.

All rights reserved. No part of this book may be reproduced or transmitted in any form or by any means, electronic or mechanical, including photocopying, recording, or by any information storage and retrieval system without the written permission of the copyright owner, and where permitted by law. Reviewers may quote brief passages in a review.

TABLE OF CONTENTS

CHAPTER ONE
IN WHICH A MARRIAGE IS PROPOSED
~09~

CHAPTER TWO
IN WHICH ALPHONSE RESIGNS HIMSELF TO MARRIAGE
~37~

CHAPTER THREE
IN WHICH ALPHONSE IS ENSNARED IN BETROTHALMENT BY ONE MISS AALIYAH KADDOUR
~49~

CHAPTER FOUR
A CONVERSATION IN THE WATERLILY HOUSE OF KEW GARDENS
~75~

CHAPTER FIVE
WHEREIN ALPHONSE FALLS OFF A HORSE AND INTO A HEDGE
~90~

CHAPTER SIX
IN WHICH ALPHONSE IS VERY MUCH UNDER THE INFLUENCE OF BOTH LOVE AND QUESTIONABLE HERBAL REMEDIES
~111~

CHAPTER SEVEN
AN UNCOMFORTABLE CONVERSATION IN WHICH TOO MUCH IS LEFT UNSAID
~132~

CHAPTER EIGHT
IN WHICH ALPHONSE IS TALKED OFF A LEDGE
~143~

CHAPTER NINE
THE DINNER PARTY, OR, A MEETING OF MINDS
~161~

CHAPTER TEN
THE NECESSARY INTIMACIES INHERENT IN BATHTIME
~179~

CHAPTER ELEVEN
IN WHICH CERTAIN DREAMS ARE FINALLY DISCUSSED
~193~

CHAPTER TWELVE
AN OLD-FASHIONED EXCHANGING OF RINGS AND VOWS
~209~

CHAPTER THIRTEEN
OR, THAT WHICH IS ALSO KNOWN AS AN EPILOGUE
~227~

THE BACHELOR'S VALET

CHAPTER ONE

IN WHICH A MARRIAGE IS PROPOSED

Alphonse Hollyhock was a golden-haired thing with guileless, cornflower-blue eyes and a good temper. His only shortcoming was a lamentable lack of grey matter, which he took in stride, cheerfully proclaiming that while he might not have two brain cells to rub together, he was dim enough that he didn't notice their lack. Thankfully, he could rely on his breeding and status to compensate. He had wealth, good looks, a broad social circle, and a nice flat in a fashionable part of London. All he lacked, according to his mother, was a wife.

"I'm sorry, I must have misheard you. You want me to do what? With whom?"

Estellabeth Hollyhock levelled him with an unimpressed glare over the rim of her porcelain teacup. Her hair was as pale as sun-bleached wheat and her eyes as flat and grey as the London sky, though otherwise, she looked much like her son—if all the life had been drained out of him. He had accepted her invitation to brunch at the estate, which he should have known was a trap, and had regretted his decision from the moment he set foot over the threshold. They were set up in the conservatory, just the two of them: a little nook overlooking the back garden, thriving with potted plants and hanging flower baskets. It was a deceptively tropical place, and, like a jungle cat, his mother had waited until her prey was comfortably settled and nibbling on jam biscuits before pouncing and digging her claws into his tender flesh.

"I can't possibly marry," he protested. "Why, a woman— I don't— There simply isn't—"

"You will, and there is. You're the perfect age for it. All your friends are engaged."

"Some of my friends have been engaged for years! And the rest have been engaged to three or four different girls in the last six months. The only one with any hope of actually seeing a marriage at the end of it is Darius Featherstrop, but that's a case of true love, if you can believe it. You can't count him."

"I do count him," she said firmly, "and you ought to be looking to him as an example, even if you can't manage to fall in love yourself. You're nearly thirty, for heaven's sake."

"I'm only twenty-six. Besides which, there are plenty of respectable bachelors well past the age of thirty."

Her mouth thinned into such an intimidatingly small line that Alphonse trembled, his teacup clacking against its saucer. He set both down on the table between them in the futile hope that she wouldn't notice his nerves.

Clearing his throat, he said, "Fine. I take it you've already set your sights on some poor girl?"

"Miss Aaliyah Kaddour. Her family owns a silk-trading empire."

Alphonse furrowed his brow. He vaguely remembered meeting an Aaliyah Kaddour at a party the previous summer: the image of a charming young woman flashed through his mind, all dusky skin and sparkling eyes, with bright flowers in her hair. She had seemed to tolerate him well enough, as far as he could recall. But he couldn't recall much, on account of having had imbibed somewhat more heavily than intended, as was often the case with such parties.

"I don't suppose she has any more say in the matter than I?"

"She's agreed to see you, which is more than I had hoped. Since you refuse to show any interest in the fairer sex and entrap a mate by more conventional means, I must rely on your money and good looks to snare you one. The latter won't last forever, and the former, I fully expect you to gamble away in some ill-placed bet with your peers in those infernal clubs." She raised one finger, warningly. "Don't think I don't know how much you lost last month betting on those useless horses at the tracks."

Alphonse swallowed his protest. He always had terrible luck with the horses and everyone knew it.

"Therefore, time is of the essence," his mother continued, as if she hadn't interrupted herself, "and I won't have you wasting any more of it."

He heaved a mournful sigh, fully aware that it wouldn't garner him an ounce of sympathy. "But I'm happy living life unwed and unshackled. Doesn't my happiness count for anything?"

"Certainly not. Now: she's coming to dinner this Friday. Have your man choose your outfit. You need to wear something nice, and you're hopeless at dressing yourself. And Alphonse." She fixed him with a steely look that would make lesser men quaver. "If you try to sabotage this in any way—if I catch so much as a whiff of some hare-brained scheme to set this astray—then I shall have no choice but to engage my backup plan, and believe me when I say that you will care for that even less than the first." She held his gaze until he was sweating from nervous anticipation. "If you don't do your utmost to procure an engagement from this girl, you shall be cut off, not only from the inheritance, but from the entire estate. Do you understand? It's well past time for you to grow up."

Alphonse went faint, the blood fleeing his face until he was as white as a sheet. "Really, Mother, surely that's a bit drastic—"

"Then an engagement should pale in comparison." She took a sip of tea without breaking eye contact. "Now, call in your man, will you? I want him to hear this in my own words, so you can't try to weasel your way out of it."

Alphonse groaned, but obediently turned to the door. Before he could so much as open his mouth, his valet stepped inside with seemingly telepathic efficiency. He entered the room, sleek and silent, his uniform black from tip to toe, to stand behind Alphonse's chair, awaiting instruction.

Jacobi had been like that for as long as he had been in Alphonse's employ. While it was natural to expect a valet to have a certain inherent sense of good timing, Jacobi's bordered on the preternatural, and if Alphonse didn't know better, he might suspect the man of using magic. Not that it was illegal for valets to use magic, but it was acknowledged to be in somewhat bad taste for the serving class to show it off, and Jacobi could never be accused of anything resembling bad taste.

"Jacobi." Alphonse's mother wore a smile for the first time all morning. Alphonse was privately certain that she would prefer if Jacobi were her son instead, class difference aside. "You heard all that, I presume?"

He inclined his head. "Yes, ma'am."

"Then you understand the importance of Friday's dinner going well. Don't let Alphonse squirm his way out of it."

"No, ma'am."

She settled back in her chair and waved her hand dismissively, as regal as a queen. "That will be all, then. Help yourself to a biscuit on your way out."

Dutifully, Jacobi selected one from the plate. Alphonse rose with a huffy sigh, sidling around the little table to press a kiss to his mother's cheek.

"Oh, don't make such a fuss," she said. "You'll thank me for this, one day."

"Yes, Mother." Turning his back to her to face Jacobi, Alphonse rolled his eyes expansively. Jacobi's expression never wavered as he held the door for him to depart.

As soon as they were on the other side with it securely shut behind them, Alphonse let out a strangled burst of frustration, striding quickly through the long halls of the house.

"Can you believe that? Marrying! Me! And to Aaliyah Kaddour, of all people!"

"Do you dislike her, sir?" Jacobi kept pace one stride behind him as they made for the front doors.

"Not at all. But that's just it! I barely know the girl. What if I come to dislike her, the more we talk? Or, more likely, she comes to dislike me? We don't know anything about one another apart from our names, and we're to be engaged in less than a week!"

"Matches of such a nature are hardly unusual, sir."

Alphonse snorted and waved him away. "Hardly unusual. It's hardly mandatory, though, is it? I was perfectly happy in my bachelorhood, I'll have you know. I had everything just the way I liked it, and I was rather looking forward to continuing on in that manner for the foreseeable future. What on earth do I need a wife for?"

"Presumably to carry on the family name, sir."

THE BACHELOR'S VALET

Alphonse pushed through the heavy front doors and onto the walkway. The Hollyhock estate was a grand old house in the countryside, sprawling over acres of green, hilly land, with gardens all around and a pond further back. Alphonse had been content there as a child, but as an adult, it seemed to look on him with as much disapproval as his mother, and he liked to escape its glower as quickly as possible. His car, a fashionable, state-of-the-art type of thing, was parked at the end of the drive, as near the gate as possible, and he headed for it with single-minded intent, Jacobi close at his heels.

"The family name will carry on just fine on its own. I've got more cousins than I can count; surely one or two of them will be happy to step up." He pulled the car door open with more aggression than was normally found in his body, flinging himself into the passenger seat.

"Your mother likely wants to see grandchildren from you, sir."

"Grandchildren! Sticky little monsters, the lot of them. If it's just a matter of her entering a broody phase, I'll wait it out. It's probably cyclical; by this time next year, she'll have moved onto some other way to torment me."

"I suppose that's possible, sir."

Alphonse crossed his arms, well aware that he was acting like a petulant child, but unable to stop himself. "Can't you offer any hope at all, Jacobi? I'm in need of a silver lining. Or, better yet, some means of escape."

"Unless you manage to make yourself so off-putting to Miss Kaddour that she withdraws her interest, I fail to see one," Jacobi said apologetically, taking the driver's seat and turning the engine to life.

It came to with a cough before settling into a rumbling purr, the kind that normally warmed Alphonse to his bones. His car was his pride and joy: shiny and black, with a great chrome grill and enough style to be the talk of the town. If he had a wife and children, he would have to give it up for something safer and slower and less fashionable. He wrinkled his nose at the thought.

Alphonse had long relied on his own personal failings to keep him from marriage, and wasn't sure how to get out of such a direct approach. Generally, women were happy to avoid topics of courtship, marriage, or love with him. He was perfectly pleasant to be around, or such was his impression: he had plenty of gentleman friends and got along with all their sisters and cousins and seasonal flings. Even Darius Featherstrop's fiancée liked him well enough. There was nothing off-putting in his manners that had women skirting around him. He simply wasn't interested in procuring a wife, or indeed anything else. And even a woman most desperate for an engagement appreciated a little amorous attention, which to Alphonse, it simply never occurred to offer.

And then there was the matter of his magic. Or, rather, lack thereof.

Every gentleman was expected to know a few basic charms and dazzlements at the bare minimum, and some turned scholarly and learned a great deal more. It was even becoming fashionable for women to learn a handful of spells to show off to their friends, and of course no party was complete without a showcase of the host's talent.

Alphonse was absolutely miserable at it. He hadn't a spark of innate talent and no amount of schooling had ever penetrated his pretty blond head, leaving him with an embarrassing dearth of tricks with which to woo a girl. While his peers flashed their magic around like birds of paradise dancing for their mates, Alphonse was left sitting in the corner nursing a drink, quite entirely by himself. Which, for the most part, suited his purposes just fine, though he could do without the vague sense of shame.

"Of course," Jacobi continued, pulling past the gate and onto the open stretch of country road, "if you did alienate Miss Kaddour, your mother would suspect you of sabotage, and I fear she is quite serious in her threats to cut you off."

"She can't possibly disown me! Why, look at me, Jacobi. How can she expect me to earn an honest living on my own? Especially here in London! Everyone knows me. I'd be a laughing stock. No: I'd have to leave the country and her nefarious interference once and for all. I'd go to—to America, perhaps. There's plenty of respectable self-made men in America, and I should have a fighting chance to start afresh. What do you say, Jacobi? Shall we book two tickets and make our way across the ocean as free men?"

"Though charmed by the prospect, sir, I do not have any particular wish to travel to America, and I must point out that were you to quit the estate, before or after being disinherited, you would lose all means by which to keep me on your payroll."

"Damn it all. I suppose you're right."

They drove in silence for some time, the only sound the rumbling growl of the engine and the pavement under their wheels. The countryside provided a charming view, all green hills and rolling pastures, but Alphonse took little delight in it.

"Sir, if I may…"

Jacobi paused, awaiting permission to continue. Valets were a particular breed of servant given to taking liberties that the common maid or housekeeper would never dream, and Jacobi was no exception. Though, admittedly, Alphonse gave him a very long leash. He rather enjoyed the liberties Jacobi took, the subtle ways in which he talked back and the less subtle ways in which he occasionally ignored, if not outright disobeyed, orders. Alphonse let him get away with it all for the sole reason that Jacobi had never yet steered him wrong. He was more than happy to let the man run his life, provided his life turned out the better for it. Thus far, in the five years he had had Jacobi, things had been altogether pleasant. And, as his mother would say, he was absolutely hopeless at running his own life, so he might as well turn the reins over to someone more competent.

"Is there any specific reason you are so opposed to marrying Miss Kaddour, or is it the thought of marriage in general that you find chafing?"

"Yes, that one. Chafing is just the word for it. I'm happy with my flat and my car and you taking care of things. I don't want a big house to look after, and I don't want to get rid of my car, and I don't see any reason at all to replace you with a woman. I'm entirely comfortable just the way I am, and I don't see why I should bend over backwards to appease my mother when it's only going to make me miserable."

"You don't know that it will make you miserable. You might find that you very much like Miss Kaddour."

Alphonse sniffed.

Jacobi was quiet as he took them around a wide bend in the road, and then: "Is it women in general, sir?"

"What about women?"

"You've never seemed especially taken with any in the time I've known you. Your friends have all fallen in and out of love more times than one can count, but you have maintained an impressive air of disinterest, if I may observe, sir."

"I suppose I just have better things to do. It seems so terribly inconvenient to be running about like that all the time, like a chicken with its head cut off. Some of my friends have been engaged on and off to the same girl for years! It's all a bit of nonsense, if you ask me. I'd much rather keep my independence, thank you very much."

"Quite right, sir," Jacobi said mildly, never taking his eyes from the road.

The drive evened out and the buildings stood closer together as they neared the city, the emerald hills flattening and giving way to houses and courtyards instead of estates and farms. Alphonse was a city boy through and through, much preferring clubs and businesses to fields and ponds, and he enjoyed the constant crush of company and never-ending bustle of humanity to the solitary introspection of the countryside. If there was one occupation he disliked, it was introspection. In fact, he made a point of avoiding it whenever possible, and while his friends were generally happy to let him be—most of them as cheerfully oblivious to their inner workings as he to his—Jacobi was less so. Alphonse doubted the man would drop the matter of women and marriage, especially not when they were so conveniently trapped together in the car.

Jacobi steered them into the city proper, the car rumbling along as the roads widened and filled with traffic.

"Out with it, then," Alphonse said, at great length. "You have that expression on your face: I know the one. The one that means you want to pry into all the nooks and crannies of my life."

"Certainly not, sir."

"I may not be the sharpest tool in the shed, but I know what your face looks like."

"I have no intention of making you uncomfortable, sir."

THE BACHELOR'S VALET

Jacobi's tone indicated that he wouldn't be pushed into speaking any further. It was a tone with which Alphonse was intimately familiar, so he sighed and leaned his temple against the window, watching the city whoosh by.

Alphonse's flat was situated on the west side of Portman Square, where he had lived for the past seven years, even before taking on Jacobi's employment. The building's facade was clean and white, a good ten storeys high, with wrought iron balconies and hanging baskets of bright flowers at every window, even in the throes of autumn. The Square housed beneath it a spacious parking garage, and the rooms were wired up with the very forefront of electric technology and a hot water system of which he had yet to encounter a shortage. It was, all in all, the very pinnacle of fashionable housing: expensive, certainly, but money had never been an issue before. His stomach dropped to think of it becoming one should he refuse to marry.

"Steak for dinner tonight, sir?" Jacobi asked, as they rode the lift to their rooms. The operator stood stoically by the door, long accustomed to the back-and-forth between the two, and too professional to show any interest, besides.

Alphonse had no real preference, largely due to Jacobi's exceptional skill in the kitchen that ensured every ingredient in whose direction he so much as glanced would be rendered delectable the instant it was put on a plate.

"Oh, whatever you like. Only, nothing too extravagant; I think this morning's conversation might have put me off my feed."

"A simple rice and vegetable dish, perhaps?"

Alphonse cast him an affronted look. "I'm not a rabbit." Though of course, they both knew he would eat whatever Jacobi set in front of him.

"A spot of tea and toast?" Jacobi suggested, perfectly straight-faced.

"Between you and my mother, I'm going to waste away into a shrivelled husk of my former self. And while I know she's quite incapable of feeling remorse, or, indeed, any sympathetic human emotion, I expect you to take your fair share in the responsibility of my untimely passing."

"Steak it is then, sir."

"Very good."

The lift came to a stop at the tenth floor, and the operator slid the ornate gold gate open for them to pass through. Alphonse flashed him a bright, if distracted smile, and the operator doffed his cap, expressionless.

Dinner was generally a casual affair, and would have been more casual still if Jacobi were less damnably stubborn. He refused to eat with Alphonse no matter how often he was invited, or how often Alphonse loudly, and at great length, spoke of how little he cared for the strict boundaries set between young gentlemen and their valets. As flexible as his manners may be in almost every other situation, there were some few rules Jacobi absolutely would not break.

He would, however, bend them.

THE BACHELOR'S VALET

Most evenings, Alphonse chattered to him as Jacobi went in and out of the kitchen, preparing dessert or washing dishes or ironing Alphonse's clothes for the next day, or whatever else needed to be done. Alphonse was perfectly capable of carrying on a conversation one-sided, and thus Jacobi was rarely required to offer more than an attentive hum every few minutes, but that evening, Alphonse was uncharacteristically quiet, and let Jacobi work undisturbed. He couldn't distract his mind from his mother's threats, nor, perhaps more aggravatingly, from his ensuing conversation with Jacobi in the car. The steak was cooked to tender perfection, the spears of asparagus crisp in their bed of lemon-butter sauce on the side, yet he found little enjoyment in his food. It was as he had suspected: the sudden stress had ruined his appetite.

But his mother wasn't present to take the blame, so his attention turned to Jacobi's unasked question from the car, looking it over from all directions, trying to puzzle out what it could have been. There were few things that caused Jacobi to hold his tongue, at least when they were alone together. In fact, Alphonse could scarcely recall the last time his valet had refused to voice an opinion in private.

But it seemed a mighty shame to let such good cooking go to waste, so he chased his food around the plate with increasing despondency until Jacobi gently cleared his throat from the doorway.

"Sir. Shall I take your plate?"

Alphonse sighed. "I suppose you'd better. Unless you'd like to take a seat and keep me company while I finish?" he added hopefully. "My brain's in such a state, perhaps if it were distracted with some conversation rather than letting it run in circles, I could eat."

But Jacobi merely fixed him with the familiar, disapproving furrowing of his brows that he engaged every time Alphonse suggested they eat together, so Alphonse set his cutlery down and let him clear the table.

"I'm going to have an early night. Perhaps when I wake up tomorrow morning, I'll find this entire day to have been an unfortunate dream."

"Perhaps, sir."

"You don't think it likely, do you."

"Not very, sir, no."

♦ ♦ ♦

Alphonse's mood did not improve after he was in bed. He tried to read a book, but found he couldn't concentrate on the words. Even the most swashbuckling of adventures failed to capture his interest. He put a record on, changed his mind, and swapped it for another, but all the songs wanted to tell him about young love, either passionate or yearning, and he wanted none of that. Finally, he wound up back under the covers swamped in restless nostalgia, trying to puzzle out whether he had ever felt the kind of love described in songs and novels. The closest he could come were his giddy school day romps with Darius Featherstrop, but that couldn't be the same sort of love everyone else was always going on about. That was just some confused schoolboy infatuation, a phase all boys went through and then grew out of.

"Well, he grew out of it, anyway," he said to his book, morosely turning the little paperback over in his hands.

A tap sounded at the door, followed by Jacobi poking his head around the frame. "Did you need anything, sir? I thought I heard your voice."

"Just musing aloud, Jacobi," Alphonse assured him. "Reminiscing about bygone years and all that. You know the sort of thing that creeps up on you in the small hours, waylaying you with memories you've not thought of in—oh, however long it's been. I'll be thinking about my childhood nanny, next!"

"Might I offer any assistance, sir?"

"Oh, no. That's quite alright," Alphonse said, though he did in fact wish Jacobi would stay to provide some company. But Jacobi was off the clock, and Alphonse couldn't monopolize the man's time just because he was feeling a bit lonely. "It's the middle of the night. You are entitled to your time off, you know, and I'd hate to impose on that."

Jacobi stepped into the room properly. "As a matter of fact, I had thought to temporarily extend my services, sir. I was thinking on your request from dinner, asking me to take your mind off your current troubles, and I regret refusing you. I expect you will find the immediate future challenging, whether you propose to Miss Kaddour or not, and I would like to be there for you. In a professional capacity, of course."

"Really? You'd do that?"

"Certainly, sir. Your wellbeing is important to me."

"In that case, I suppose a small distraction would be just the thing. Why don't you tell me what all that was about in the car earlier, then?"

Jacobi glanced away. "I hardly think it appropriate, sir," he demurred, which only piqued Alphonse's curiosity further.

"Oh, go on! You've got some sort of insight, I can see it. And you know if you never tell me, I'll certainly never work it out on my own. I'm hopeless at that sort of thing."

"You're perfectly capable of insight, sir. This would be nothing more than indulging my own curiosity, which is, as I say, inappropriate."

"A heap of nonsense," Alphonse said firmly. "I've known you for five years, Jacobi, and I can't imagine you asking me any question I'd be reluctant to answer."

"You frequently refuse to answer my questions, sir."

"Well, alright, when you ask me things like what's happened to my least favourite suit, or why I gave away that one bit of antique furniture, or, or the bit about that parrot I brought home that one time—"

"So you admit, you did intentionally bring that parrot onto the premises, sir?"

"But," Alphonse continued doggedly, "not once have I refused to answer anything pertaining to my personal life, and I stand by that. So, go on and ask it, whatever it is. It's the middle of the night and you're not even supposed to be working. Let's just say that whatever conversation happens now, it doesn't count, what?"

Jacobi levelled Alphonse with a studious look, seeming to get right inside his brainpan in a way that, coming from anyone else, would have been mightily discomforting, before finally acquiescing. "I inferred from our earlier conversation that you have not been with a woman, sir."

"Been with?"

"Intimately, sir."

"Ah. Intimately. Well, no, I've not *intimately* been with a woman, in that sense, no."

It wasn't as awful saying such a thing to Jacobi as it would have been to his friends. Alphonse felt few of the same social pressures in private company as he did in the clubs. There were times when it seemed that his peers were little better than a pack of hyenas, eager to tear into some fresh and tender prey, and laughing at their conquests all the while. Jacobi, in contrast, was as a lion: noble, and far less inclined to crude judgement. Then again, having never explored the safari nor met either of the beasts in question, Alphonse may be accused of anthropomorphising the poor creatures. Perhaps hyenas were jolly good companions that would never shame a man for his lack of sexual expertise. He couldn't really say.

"And not out of respect for holy matrimony, I take it."

"Oh, no, nothing like that. I don't know many chaps who have the patience for that sort of thing. Girls neither, really. It's quite old fashioned, isn't it? Hardly the style anymore."

"As you say, sir. If I may ask you further—"

"Do go on."

"Are you disinterested in the notion of sex and romance altogether, then, or merely disinterested in women, sir?"

Alphonse hardly knew what to say to that. "Well, one naturally leads to the other, doesn't it?"

Jacobi looked at him for a long moment. "Then you're not interested in men, sir?" he finally asked.

"*Interested* is a strong word," Alphonse floundered, feeling himself going red. "Just as disinterested is a bit strong. In sex, I mean. I do know my way around the mechanics of the thing, after all. For heaven's sake, I'm twenty-six, man."

Jacobi looked at him unwaveringly. He was unwavering in all things, come to think: like a Greek statue, and every bit as pleasing to behold. Alphonse suspected that he needn't even blink, save for keeping up appearances.

"What I mean to say," Alphonse continued hastily, before he could ruminate any more on the particulars of African wildlife or Greek statuary, "is that I've had some manner of sexual encounters before, yes, with men. As a sort of juvenile experience, what? Why, you don't get through university without having tried a thing or two. You put a bunch of bright young men together in such an environment, it's only natural to experiment some, but it's not the sort of thing to be carried into adulthood."

"Might I infer that your experiences were thus contained entirely to your school days, sir?"

THE BACHELOR'S VALET

"Well, there may have been an incident or two—or three, rather, or perhaps a handful more, but who's really counting—in the clubs, you know. After a few drinks with the lads, things can get— But it's nothing serious. Just blowing off steam, as it were. It's not the same as really…you know. Doing the deed." He waggled his eyebrows meaningfully, hoping that Jacobi would save him from having to go on. When Jacobi merely looked at him, Alphonse took a deep breath and ploughed forth. "Two friends can have a spot of kissing and lend a hand once or twice without it being, well." He dropped his voice, as if there were anyone else present who might overhear them. "It's not exactly buggery, is it? And if feelings of a slightly more amorous nature get involved, that's easily put down to the confusing age of it, what? The hormones of youth, and all that." He nodded decisively, even as the unbidden memory of Darius Featherstrop, with his perfect swoop of copper-brown hair, rose to the forefront of his mind. "Nothing indecent about it."

"No, sir. I never meant to suggest anything of the sort." Jacobi cleared his throat softly. "When you put your feelings down to the hormones of youth, sir. Did you have romantic notions for your fellows at the time?"

Alphonse buried his hands under the bedcovers, suddenly feeling very small. "I had thought he and I had feelings for each other, which was silly, of course. Boys aren't supposed to get that way with each other, and I was… I was confused, is all."

"Sir," Jacobi said gently. "There is nothing unusual in two men developing feelings for one another that go deeper than those of mere sexual gratification. Nor in two women developing such feelings, for that matter. Same-sex relationships have the potential for as much romance as any man and woman paired together. And, if I may add, sir, it's far more common than society would have you believe."

Alphonse paused, dry-mouthed and heart thumping at Jacobi's words. The sorts of feelings he meant were very much wrapped up in the physical, for at that age, everything was physical, often at rather inconvenient moments. And in hindsight, they did sound an awful lot like how his friends described their feelings for whatever poor girls had caught their attention that month, and had more than a bit in common with those crooning love songs, too. Naturally, his feelings for Featherstrop had gone nowhere, for though they had shared a great number of intimacies during university, that sort of thing simply wasn't done. Featherstrop had moved on, and Alphonse had somehow been left behind in the dust.

"Men can fall in love with other men," he said wonderingly, unsure if he meant it as a question or a statement.

"Indeed, sir."

"Well. You know, Jacobi, you might be onto something with that."

"Indeed, sir?"

"I suppose I was rather in love with him. I hadn't thought of it that way before. You are sharp, aren't you?"

"I try my best, sir."

"Have you ever been in love?" Alphonse asked plaintively.

"Once, yes, sir."

"I suppose it didn't end in sunshine and roses, what with you working for me like this. Ah, sorry, old chap. What a dratted inconsiderate thing of me to ask. Pretend I never said anything, what?"

"It's quite alright, sir. You are correct to observe that I am not married." Jacobi paused, as if searching for the right words. It was one of the things that Alphonse liked most about him: his careful consideration of every phrase that left his mouth. Alphonse hadn't the forethought to manage anything half so elegant. "I never pursued it, sir. It was an inappropriate match."

"Unrequited love, eh? That's a sorry thing."

"I believed it was unrequited at the time, though I do occasionally wonder if I should have made my feelings known more plainly."

"Any chance of rekindling the old spark?" Alphonse asked optimistically. "Provided the girl is still around, no reason not to make those feelings known now. Better late than never, and all that!"

"Perhaps," Jacobi allowed, with a politely neutral smile that suggested that, while he appreciated his master's input, he would do no such thing.

"Say no more." Alphonse had barely paused a second before asking, "But have you never given thought to pursuing the old married life in general?"

"I have sir, and I may say with some confidence that it is not for me."

"No? I must admit, I'm glad to hear it. I should hate to lose you, you know. It would be quite a bother to find a new valet of your calibre."

"Thank you, sir."

"But might I ask why not? It can't be wanting to avoid the commitment. You're as loyal as— Well, I was going to say a dog, but that sounds rather derogatory, now that I come to think it. You are loyal, though. Endlessly so! Anyone should be lucky to have you as a husband."

"Thank you, sir," Jacobi repeated, with more amusement this time. "But it's simply not of interest to me. I enjoy my work, and the hours are such that I could not continue in your service and be of any company to a spouse. Therefore, I find it a simple choice to remain here."

Alphonse was relieved. Though he wanted his man to be happy—indeed, he wanted him to be as happy as any man could be, for Jacobi deserved the world and more—he had to admit to the shudder of terror at the thought of Jacobi leaving him on his lonesome to pursue wedded bliss. Making his way through life in the clutches of some lesser valet simply didn't bear thinking about.

"You'll stay on if I get married, though, won't you? I know many valets prefer bachelors; I suppose a wife might take offense to you running her husband's life when that ought to be her job. But I simply don't know what I'd do without you."

"It would depend very much on the manner of woman you were to marry. But rest assured, sir, if I were to leave your employ, I should take it upon myself to find you a suitable replacement."

"I can't imagine one exists," Alphonse said, glumly. "Isn't there anything I can do to persuade you to stay?"

Jacobi hesitated. "Sir…"

Wincing, Alphonse took it all back. "Sorry, sorry. What a drattedly uncouth thing to say, eh?" He shook his head. "Forget I said anything. Wasn't thinking. Just—" He waved his hand. "As you were." When Jacobi only looked at him, a shimmer of concern marring his otherwise smooth and perfect brow, Alphonse forced a smile. "Jolly impractical to imagine myself a bachelor forever, what? And unrealistic to think I could keep you by my side all my life. The inexorable march of time, and whatnot."

"Sir," Jacobi tried again.

"I'm being maudlin," Alphonse said firmly. "It was all that fresh country air this morning; it must have muddled my brain. Don't you fret: I'll get some sleep and be right as rain come morning."

"As you say. Good night, sir."

"Good night, Jacobi," Alphonse said, and dropped his head back to his pillow, determined to banish all troublesome thoughts of marriage and abandonment from his mind.

♦ ♦ ♦

Alphonse dreamed of the little cottage house again.

Or at least, he assumed he had dreamed of it before. It had the same familiarity as a childhood memory, or a spot of déjà vu: hazy around the edges, but undeniably recognisable, like one of those tunes they always played at the music halls where he knew the melody, but not the name or the words. It was a quaint little place, though not the sort he'd have chosen himself, either in dreams or real estate. It was a shade too rustic for his tastes, with the ceiling beams exposed and a host of rose bushes climbing the stones of the outside wall. Like a watercolour painting from a fairy tale rather than the sharp marble-and-gold fashion he'd have for his own home.

That said, Alphonse was fond of his little cottage dream. Nothing bad ever happened in it, in contrast to his usual dreams, which were often filled with nonsense capers or flashbacks to his university exams. He had one recurring dream about trying to drive his car through a flooded London street as the cab slowly filled with upset fish, and he could say with confidence that he preferred the cottage.

Wandering through the kitchen, with its shiny pots and pans and bunches of dried herbs hanging from the ceiling, he stepped through the back door and into the garden. It was a perfect summer evening, which was how he knew it wasn't real. The real England was firmly in autumn's grip, and besides, it was the kind of perfect that London never really got: lush grass warm underfoot, the sunset lighting up the treetops with swathes of pink and purple, the air just the right temperature to be out in shirtsleeves without catching a chill or working up a sweat.

At his approach, Jacobi glanced up from the back of the garden where he was lounging in a low chair with a grey-and-brown striped tabby purring in his lap. Hanging low in the air around him, bobbing sedately and emitting a soft, pale gold glow, were orbs of light like paper lanterns. Alphonse knew with the kind of unquestioning knowledge that only comes in dreams that they were Jacobi's magic, and one of them drifted over to him in silent greeting. Alphonse held out one hand as one might greet a friendly animal, and it bopped along his fingertips, soft as a cloud, before returning to its master, leaving a bright, summery scent like fresh citrus in its wake.

"Hullo," Alphonse said, slinging his hands in his pockets. "I see your friend's come back."

The cat opened her pale green eyes to blink at him slowly before turning her face back into Jacobi's hand to be petted. She was as familiar as everything else about the cottage, though Alphonse had no idea where she came from or what she was called.

"I think she'd let you pet her if you tried."

"Oh, no. She looks so comfortable as she is, I wouldn't want to muddle that up."

"She'll get up when we go in for tea anyway," Jacobi pointed out.

"True enough, I just—" Alphonse stopped short. From over the garden wall came a thin, chilling cry that gripped him in icy terror. "Say, do you hear that?"

"Hm?"

"It sounds like Mother's calling me."

"I don't hear anything."

"Ugh, I'd best go see what she wants. Nothing good, I'm sure."

"Shall I set a plate for you?"

"Yes, I don't expect this will take a moment. You really can't hear that? Like the wailing of winter wind, a gnashing of maternal teeth? Perhaps she hits a frequency only her own offspring can hear. Like a dog whistle, or some such."

Shaking his head, Alphonse trekked to the little wooden gate and squeezed through, tipping his head from one side to the other, trying to pinpoint the direction of that call. The moment he left the garden and its summer rosebud embrace, the cottage shimmered out of his mind like a mirage, and his subconscious filled up the empty space with hazy nonsense until he slipped into a deeper sleep, and the dream faded away entirely.

CHAPTER TWO

IN WHICH ALPHONSE RESIGNS HIMSELF TO MARRIAGE

When morning came, Alphonse did not find himself right as rain. To the contrary: his mood remained uncharacteristically under the weather, and half-formed memories of a dream danced around his brain, teasing him with glimpses of things he couldn't clearly recall. Jacobi had been involved, he was sure, but he couldn't get the gist of it except that being bereft of that dream and whatever company it had involved left him strangely mournful and nostalgic, like he was missing out on something grand by simple virtue of having woken.

He thus determined that the best course of action would be to go out, surround himself with sympathetic company, and drink until he cheered up again. He was generally a cheerful drunk, as he was generally cheerful in all states, and though some small part of his brain suggested that drinking wouldn't solve the problem, he shut that part away (ignoring that it sounded suspiciously like Jacobi) and forged on without it.

"I don't think I've ever seen you look so down before," Morgan Hollyhock observed as Alphonse oozed into the chair beside him at the Stag's Head, immediately dropping his head in his hands.

The Stag's Head had been established in Victorian times, and hadn't changed its fashion much since then. Everything was walnut and chestnut and bronze and gold, the wood panels of the walls dark and quiet, the chair legs and round table tops polished to a warm glow. It was a friendly, cosy atmosphere on most days, filled to the brim with lively chaps young and old looking to while away their hours away from home. Alphonse had practically grown up in the place, and it rarely failed to lift his spirits, either through company, alcohol, or the mere distraction of his peers. Unfortunately, he suspected that a looming marriage might be too much for the Stag's Head to defeat.

"I've never felt so down." Alphonse lifted his face just enough to peer blearily at his cousin. "How do you do it?"

"Feel down? It just comes naturally, I suppose."

"That's jolly depressing. But no, I mean, maintain your bachelorhood! You're past thirty, yet I don't see our esteemed elders beating down your door to force your hand in marriage. How do you avoid that whole mess?"

"I suppose I'm too boring for them to bother with," Morgan said, after a moment's consideration.

"I wouldn't say boring. Studious, perhaps. Or serious? One or both of those."

Morgan shrugged. "The point is, I haven't exhibited any traits they feel need correcting, so I'm more or less left to my own devices."

"I don't need correcting!" Alphonse said indignantly. "Just because I like to lay a few bets on the ponies and indulge in a few drinks here and there, that doesn't mean…" He swallowed. "Should I strive to be more boring, do you think?"

"I think it's a bit late for that, if your mother is already lining up potential wives."

"But I could still turn over a new leaf. Couldn't I?"

Morgan sighed and turned to face him. "Alphonse. Look."

Alphonse looked, desperately.

"You're a naturally frivolous man. Like a butterfly, flitting from one thing to the next, your head as empty as the flowers it lands on. There's nothing wrong with having all the depth of a ball of tissue paper, but playing a serious role? No one will buy it, and you'll make yourself miserable trying."

"You're not wrong."

"Anyway, that's what you've got Jacobi for. He's the brains of the operation; you're just the window dressing. I hope I'm not offending you," Morgan added, as if in afterthought.

"Oh, not at all. I rather like butterflies, in fact. They do seem to lead such happy, simple little lives." Alphonse sank his head back into his hands. "Of course, they only live a few days, so I can't imagine they've got monstrous dragons of mothers breathing down their necks, egging them on to mate faster."

"No, I shouldn't think so." Morgan offered him a conciliatory pat on the back. "Sorry, but I think you're in for it, this time. Better buck up and make the best of it."

Alphonse peeled himself up off the table. "Morgan, old chap. I don't know the first thing about women, let alone marriage. What am I supposed to do?"

Morgan grimaced. A more optimistic man might call it a smile, but Alphonse couldn't rouse such hope. "Learn," Morgan advised.

"Learn," Alphonse repeated. "Righto. I can learn."

Scanning the club in distress, he caught sight of Darius Featherstrop by the bar, and immediately brightened. If Alphonse had indeed been in love once before, then who better to teach him how to fall in love again than his first flame? Especially what with Featherstrop being so nauseatingly in love himself with his fiancée. If he couldn't enlighten Alphonse on the matter, then he was surely beyond all help. Slipping out of his chair and his cousin's company, Alphonse headed over to his erstwhile friend, clapping him on the back as he smiled his greetings to Featherstrop's companions.

"Hullo, Hollyhock! We were just toasting my engagement!" Featherstrop said cheerfully. He was bright-eyed and rather red in the cheeks, suggesting that this wasn't his first toast, or indeed his third.

"Oh, cheers! I'd better get the next round, shall I?"

Following a rousing cry of support and a downed round of drinks, Alphonse slung one arm around Featherstrop's shoulders and drew him away from his small crowd of well-wishers, who immediately closed in to fill his absence like he had never been there. For his part, Featherstrop amiably followed Alphonse along to an empty table where they might have a moment of private conversation.

"Featherstrop, old thing, I need to pick your brain a moment, if you can spare the grey matter."

"Pick it about what?"

"Well, the mother's decided I need marrying off post-haste, and I thought, what with you being so happy with your Lucy, maybe you could tell me how to go about it."

"How to go about what, exactly?" Featherstrop asked, bewildered.

Alphonse swallowed. "Falling in love with a girl and marrying her?"

"What!" Featherstrop exclaimed with a laugh. "Hollyhock, it's the easiest thing in the world! You only have to set your sights on a girl, and your heart will do the rest. If she rejects you, then you move on to the next. Eventually you'll find one who falls for you just as hard as you've fallen for her, and that's all there is to it!"

It did sound awfully simple, when he put it like that. "But what if my heart doesn't *want* to fall in love with a girl?"

Featherstrop looked him up and down. "Oh, you're one of those types, are you?"

Alphonse froze like a rabbit in the headlights of an overbearing car. "How do you mean?"

"I mean." Featherstrop returned his arm to its place around Alphonse's shoulders, reeling him in companionably. "I mean: one of those types so taken with his own bachelorhood that he hasn't stopped to consider the other side of the fence! It takes some vulnerability to fall in love as easily as I did, but it's so much more rewarding than just…" He flicked his fingers dismissively. "Playing the game and racking up notches in your bedpost."

"My bedpost—"

"Hollyhock." Featherstrop turned to face him head on, his hands on Alphonse's shoulders. "There are greener pastures waiting for you, old boy. If your mother wants you to marry, I say you should let it happen."

"I don't even know the girl she's got picked out for me," Alphonse protested weakly.

Featherstrop considered this. "Is she pretty?"

"I think so."

"And monied?"

"Presumably."

"And I dare say she must be cleverer than you, no offense, chap."

"Oh, none taken."

"Then meet her with an open mind and an open heart, and stop worrying so much," Featherstrop advised. "There's nothing better than being in love! You just have to, you know."

"Let it happen," Alphonse repeated. "Right." He hesitated before gathering his courage. "Say. You remember our time together at school?"

"Course I do, chap! The golden days of youth, eh? What about them?"

"Well, looking back, we never had the company of any women then, and we did alright for ourselves, didn't we? Never felt the—the lack of such feminine charm?"

"Oh, we made do with what we had."

"Was that all it was?"

Featherstrop paused, studying him in a moment of uncharacteristic sobriety. "Hollyhock, old chap, what else would it be? You can't expect that every young man who fools around in university is committing himself to a life of confirmed bachelorhood!"

The way he said it made the concept so ridiculous that Alphonse hastened to agree, though he felt rather wilted inside.

"No, of course not! I just get nostalgic, I suppose, looking back on it from time to time. It all seemed so much less bally complicated then, didn't it?"

Featherstrop laughed, and the sombre moment shattered. "Women are only as complicated as you make them! Propose to the girl and let her make you happy. My Lucy's made me the happiest man in the world, after all."

"It's just— The thing is, I was happy then, what?"

"Well, of course you were. We all were! Boys that age, we didn't have a care in the world, not a single trouble. Not a single thought, either, I dare say."

"I mean that I was happy without any female company."

"We didn't know what we were missing," Featherstrop said wistfully.

"Featherstrop!" Alphonse cried, his voice strangled. "What I mean to say is that I was fond of you, not some imagined girl. I never wanted to replace you with anyone else, feminine-figured or otherwise."

Featherstrop blinked at him owlishly and Alphonse bit his tongue, already regretting saying a word.

"Hollyhock." Featherstrop looked a bit stunned. "Hollyhock, old thing, let me give you a word of advice. What we did in university? That's the same as all schoolboys do. We explored, and we roughhoused, and we had a grand old time doing it, eh?"

"We did."

"But we were as babes in the woods back then, stumbling through life blind without anyone to guide us. What we had wasn't a relationship. It was just a bit of experimentation between two desperate, clueless chaps who didn't know any better. Do you really want to give up the chance at a proper relationship with a lovely girl for something like that? Would you really ask me to?"

Alphonse had to open and shut his mouth a few times before he could convince the words to come out.

"No," he finally managed, "no, of course not, old thing. That's not what I meant at all."

Featherstrop nodded and gave his shoulder a firm squeeze. "I should hope not."

"No, what a jolly strange..." Alphonse shook his head. "When you put it like that, what a jolly strange thing to ask of a man. I lost my head for a minute, that's all. Panicked, you see, about the suddenness of it, and getting nostalgic for. Erm. For simpler times, what?"

Featherstrop broke into a smile once more, apparently oblivious to the way Alphonse felt like the floor was dropping out from under him. "There you go. Nothing wrong with a bit of stage fright before popping the big question! But you'll come out alright in the end."

"Yes, yes, of course I will." Alphonse managed a queasy smile. "Nothing to it at all."

"Tell you what: you ought to be celebrating. Once you connect with your girl, the both of you ought to come up to the estate and have a spot of hunting, eh? You can introduce her to everyone, and we'll have a rollicking good time of it! Put you right at ease, what do you say?"

"I've never been much for hunting," he said weakly.

"That's alright. We hardly ever catch sight of the damn fox, never mind kill the thing. I'll see you there the weekend after next and we'll have a grand old time!"

"Right. I suppose that's as good a plan as any, what?"

♦ ♦ ♦

Alphonse returned home feeling worse than when he had headed out.

"Marriage seems inevitable," he said, morosely folding himself into his favourite armchair after Jacobi relieved him of his coat. "If not now, to this girl, then later, to another. Is there truly nothing to be done?"

"Given time, I'm confident I could extract you from any proposal, sir, but, as you say: if the first does not take, your mother will doubtless arrange a second. And your inheritance would be in considerable jeopardy, sir."

"So, you don't recommend me trying to wriggle my way out of it."

Jacobi hesitated. "At the moment, I must recommend that you meet Miss Kaddour. Then, if you find she is wholly unsuitable, I will concoct some scheme to remove you from her, without drawing your mother's suspicion. But I don't believe it to be a long-term solution. I think, as distasteful as you find the prospect, you must steel yourself to the idea of wedded bliss, sir."

"I suppose the prospect of finding myself penniless in the streets is worse. Once I'm wedded, you'll stay long enough for me to transition to the new horror my life's become, won't you, Jacobi? I know you said you'd find me a new valet, but please stay. Just for a month. A week! I simply wouldn't know what to do without you."

"I have no intention of abandoning you to your fate, sir," Jacobi said firmly. "But you mustn't put the cart before the horse. Meet Miss Kaddour, and then we shall determine your next course of action."

Alphonse heaved a mighty sigh. "You're right, of course. You always are. I shall be married, whether I like it or not, and all I can do is make the best of it. I just didn't expect the concept to dredge up all these other feelings. I hadn't thought about my school days in years, you know, and now I can't seem to stop thinking about them."

"There's nothing wrong with taking a moment to reflect on one's past, sir. Especially when one's present has been suddenly upended."

"I was just talking to Darius Featherstrop at the club, and it sent me into a bit of a mood. And it shouldn't have! I'm perfectly happy for him. But the way he was going on about the nature of love, like falling for a girl is as easy as flicking a switch, and the way he's never known love before his fiancée…"

"Perfectly natural for a young man on the cusp of marriage, I would think, sir."

"Yes, of course." Alphonse dropped his gaze to his hands, fiddling with the cuff of his suit. "It's just that he was one of those boys I had a thing with back at school. Nothing serious—just youthful fumblings and the like—except that it was my first time, and I did rather love him. I feel somewhat foolish having said it all aloud now. Why, a whole lifetime has passed since then, and it's not as if I've been pining for him all these years like some moonstruck girl."

"It can be difficult," said Jacobi softly, "to realise that a fond memory has been remembered differently by other parties."

Alphonse hummed. "How on earth did you come to work as a valet, Jacobi? You dispense this wisdom so effortlessly. Surely you'd be better served doing something more, well, important. Waiting on a young lord or a duke or some such."

"I have no desire to serve any dukes or lords, thank you, sir. I find myself content in your service, and will remain with you for as long as your situation allows."

"Never mind serving lords or dukes; you should be one yourself," Alphonse declared, drawing his hands over his face. "Your noble spirit is far too great to be confined to a life of this drudgery, and you can't tell me otherwise."

"You're veering into melodrama, sir. I'll fetch you a tea."

CHAPTER THREE

IN WHICH ALPHONSE IS ENSNARED IN BETROTHALMENT BY ONE MISS AALIYAH KADDOUR

Friday's dinner approached with looming inescapability, lumbering nearer by the hour as if it sought to crush Alphonse beneath its great and unsympathetic bulk.

"Are you sure you won't run away to the Americas with me?" he asked on Friday afternoon without much hope, as Jacobi systematically demolished his wardrobe in the hunt for the perfect suit.

"I'm afraid not, sir." At least he had the grace to sound apologetic. "And I cannot advise you flee the continent on your own. Do you prefer the blue or the grey suit?"

"Neither. Let me wear black, seeing as it's my funeral we're arranging."

"Grey it is, sir. May I assist you in getting dressed?"

"No, no. I'm perfectly capable of dressing myself, however useless my mother thinks me."

Alphonse flung himself over the bed, limbs akimbo as he stared forlornly at the ceiling. Jacobi laid the suit out next to him. It was a handsome thing, flattering to the form and a soft, gentle colour, but therein lay the problem: he didn't want to give this Aaliyah girl the slightest reason to find him attractive, and he certainly didn't want to look like an appealing prospect as a husband.

"Leave me to my fate, if you please."

"As you wish, sir." Jacobi bowed just low enough to seem sarcastic before sweeping from the room.

"I can dress myself," Alphonse repeated. The grey suit looked at him with judgment winking from its shiny buttons. He rolled onto his side to play with the pocket square laid atop the lapel. "I don't want to marry the girl," he told it despondently. "I don't want to marry *any* girl! What do you think, old chap? Could we survive on our own, sans estate? I could sell you for a few pounds, I should think."

The suit, which was a fine wool and silk blend befitting the autumnal chill, and had never seen him do a day's work in his life, seemed doubtful.

Alphonse shook his head and pushed himself upright, shedding the morning's casual clothes. "No, perhaps not, eh?"

THE BACHELOR'S VALET

The suit fit like a dream, of course; all his suits did. Jacobi made sure of it. And while Alphonse normally enjoyed the suits Jacobi arranged for him, fresh from the tailor and always in the height of fashion, which Alphonse could never manage on his own, he found himself scowling at his reflection rather than preening. The full-length mirror beside the wardrobe showed him a handsome young man with a slim-cut suit that seemed to say he was just dashing enough to be interesting, yet altogether a safe and respectable choice of partner.

But he didn't want to be Miss Kaddour's partner, damn it all, and he didn't want his suits to be joining ranks against him. He didn't want to don his finest plumage to strut around trying to impress the female persuasion in order to win a mate just to appease his mother. Never mind his own misery—what of the poor girl? Surely she would never be satisfied with such a husband, even if Jacobi by some miracle chose to remain in his employ to guide him through the worst of his gaffs and faux pas.

But then, there was disinheritance to consider. If his mother disowned him then he couldn't hope to secure a decent job on his own, especially without a lick of magic to ease his way. He couldn't conjure so much as a solitary flame to keep him warm in his inevitable homelessness, much less conjure up a ream of cash to support him in the manner to which he was accustomed. (He had never given much thought as to the nature of money or economy, and assumed that when one was lacking money, he could merely snap new bills into existence to rectify that mistake.) And he hadn't the head for books or numbers, which relegated him to the realm of physical labour, and that was too ghastly a life to imagine. Ghastlier than marriage, even.

But the thing that spooked him the most about such an imagined scenario was that there would be no Jacobi at his side throughout. With such a man as Jacobi, Alphonse might find the fortitude to weather any manner of storm, but without him—

No, it didn't bear thinking about.

"Righto." He smoothed down the suit's dovey lapels and looked his reflection square in the eye, forcing his expression from one of dreary melancholy to something more determined. "There's no escaping this dinner, so let's make the best of it, what, old chap?"

Nodding sharply, he lifted his chin and marched from the room to find Jacobi and begin the trek out to the grand old Hollyhock estate, where he would meet his doom head on, with all the gallantry and noble fortitude of the knights of old.

Unfortunately, his fortitude failed to survive the drive. Like a delicate summer bloom facing down the changing season, it withered, and long before they reached their destination he was already succumbing to unattractive fidgeting and great, gusty sighs that caused Jacobi to thin his lips and tighten his grip on the wheel. Alphonse wished Jacobi would say something: anything! Chide him for his childish mannerisms, or offer him some lone spark of optimism to see him through the evening. But Alphonse didn't vocalise any of those wishes, and Jacobi for once didn't seem inclined to speak out of turn, so Alphonse spent the drive in miserable silence, with nothing but the rumble of the engine to distract him.

Were the dinner party hosted by anyone other than his mother, and with any other goal than seeing him engaged, Alphonse might have had a wonderful time. There were ten guests invited, himself and Miss Kaddour included, all of them dressed to the nines and in the particular high spirits that came from a good meal, and even better wine. Alphonse alone was brimming with nervous energy, and it seemed that everyone else kept looking at him with anticipatory knowledge, as if they were all in on his mother's scheme, and were waiting for him to drop a knee and propose to the girl on the spot. Taking a gulp from his wine glass in an effort to calm his nerves, he immediately choked.

"Are you alright, Mr. Hollyhock?" Miss Kaddour asked from her seat beside him. They were all lounging casually around the dinner table awaiting dessert, sipping their drinks and talking merrily with one another. Alphonse was uncharacteristically quiet, too eaten up with nerves to chatter on as he normally did, and he jumped slightly when she addressed him.

"Oh, fine, just fine," he assured her, replacing his glass on the table. "Just took a swig down the wrong tube, I'm afraid."

Miss Kaddour was objectively beautiful, with dusky brown skin and thick, dark hair whose waves were pinned in place at the nape of her neck. Her dress hung off elegant shoulders to fall to her knees: a rich indigo blue from top to bottom, and sparkling with beads all down the front. She was as attractive a match as any man could dream of marrying, and only a fool would turn her down.

But Alphonse had always been a fool, and, try as he might, he couldn't rouse the faintest lick of attraction for her. There was no stirring of the loins, no thumping of the heart, no stuttering of the soul in her lovely presence. He had in good confidence from his peers that those were all things a man ought to feel in the company of a beautiful girl, but his body remained staggeringly disinterested.

Luckily, she was as charming a conversationalist as she was a looker, and steered her way effortlessly through the waters of dinnertime chatter without a moment's hesitation. All he had to do was make the occasional declaration of accordance or hum of interest, which he dropped in every so often between bites. And, though she made a point of including him in every topic brought her way, she never mentioned anything of a proposal, or marriage in general, nor gave any indication that she was interested in him as anything more than a spot of polite company.

Though, every once in a while, he caught her looking at him: not with the bright-eyed interest of a girl looking at a man she liked, nor the shrewd, calculating interest of a matriarch working out how best to entrap a hapless male in her schemes, but rather with a curious, studious expression, as if she were puzzling out what to make of him. He wished he could spare her the trouble and inform her, point-blank, that he had neither depths nor secrets, and that there was really nothing particularly curious or interesting about him at all, and certainly not for a girl of her nature. But he suspected that such an honest declaration would be considered an attempt to wriggle out of an engagement, and, so fearing his mother's icy glare from the head of the table, he kept his trap shut.

Still: Miss Kaddour wasn't mooning over him, not even close, and it gave him hope that his mother had perhaps misinterpreted her interest, and he might escape the evening altogether unscathed, or rather, un-betrothed.

It was, of course, overly optimistic of him. It was over dessert that his mother sprung her trap, claws extended.

"I hear you have an interest in horticulture, Miss Kaddour," she said, as the pastry chef placed a dish of carefully sculpted chocolate mousse cake before her.

"I do, Mrs. Hollyhock. It's become quite a hobby of mine."

"Then you're in luck! Our gardens are in full bloom—I have the climate controlled by the same magicks they use at Kew, you see—and I would be entirely remiss if I didn't suggest a tour. Perhaps," she said, turning to fix Alphonse with a knowing look, "you would be so kind as to show her around, after dessert?"

"Indeed," he stammered. "Of course, I should be delighted, Miss Kaddour."

"Oh, marvellous," Miss Kaddour said with a smile, laying one delicate hand on his forearm. "I've heard such flattering things about your gardens, of course, and—" She was off again, her conversation pleasantly lilting its way over the meal's final course.

But Alphonse could find no more pleasure in her words than he could in her form. Less, even, because while her physical body left him merely disinterested, her bird-like chatter, while pleasing in its musicality, left him in a cold sweat. In the gardens, he would be forced to speak with her one-on-one. What if he proposed and she said yes? What if he proposed, but his mother had read Miss Kaddour wrong, and she laughed in his face for suggesting marriage after a single evening of acquaintanceship, and then his mother disinherited him anyway? He could scarcely imagine which was worse. His chocolate raspberry mousse cake was not the foamy delight he had anticipated, but a tasteless drudge upon his tongue.

Dessert ended after an eternity, yet still too soon. Miss Kaddour rose expectantly, glancing at him with those bright, inquisitive eyes. Oh, blast—surely Jacobi could concoct some genius scheme to rescue him after all! He jolted upright without an ounce of grace.

"Excuse me, Miss Kaddour, but I really must dash to the loo. Back in a mo!"

And then he fled the dining room, careening through the hall until, panting, he discovered Jacobi near the kitchen, in idle conversation with the serving staff. Jacobi, noting the young master's panicked dishevelment, politely excused himself, allowing Alphonse to draw him into a windowed alcove.

"I can't do it," Alphonse whispered. "You've got to get me out of here. What's the plan, then?"

"I advise you propose to her," Jacobi said firmly.

Alphonse's jaw dropped, and his stomach with it. "What! That's just the opposite of a plan!"

"I have reason to believe that Miss Kaddour has motivations separate from those of your mother, and it may be in both your interests to go through with this proposal, if not the whole marriage."

"What reasons?" Alphonse demanded in a hiss.

"I'm not at liberty to say, sir."

Alphonse eyed him. "I don't like this, Jacobi."

"No, sir."

"Are they awfully good reasons, the ones you're basing these beliefs on?"

"They are, sir. And if Miss Kaddour chooses to confide in you, I believe you will find them most sympathetic."

"But you can't confide in me yourself."

"No, sir. I intruded on a private moment just prior to dinner, and I don't feel it's my place to tell her secrets before she does."

"Ever the gentleman." Alphonse huffed. "Very well, I'll do it. But if this goes wrong, Jacobi, I'll— Well, blast it all, I suppose that'll be the end of things."

"I have every faith in you, sir."

"Well, I jolly well don't. Right. Toodle-pip."

Squaring his jaw, Alphonse rounded the corner and tracked Miss Kaddour down outside the dining room, gallantly offering her his arm and trying not to visibly sweat as she accepted it and steered them outside.

It was a beautiful evening, though the magic-induced warmth did nothing to warm his innards, which were beginning to feel like the vast, frozen expanse of the Arctic Circle. Inside the bubble of temperate magic, the garden grew green and leafy, bobbing with sweet, heavy-headed blossoms: bluebells and foxgloves and buttercups and roses and all manner of other delicate, feminine blooms for which he had no names, and which only served to make him feel all the colder in comparison.

"Mr. Hollyhock," his lovely companion began.

"Alphonse, please," he garbled.

"Alphonse. Then you must call me Aaliyah, of course."

Of course; it wouldn't do to have them engaged and still spouting formalities. "Aaliyah."

She smiled and patted his arm, which was still linked gentlemanly through hers. "Alphonse. I had a whole speech planned out, but first, I really must ask: are you quite well? Because you look rather pale, and I can feel you shaking."

"I assure you, I've never felt better," he forced out through a painfully false smile. "Ah. What speech?" He didn't have a speech prepared; he was treading water without a life raft.

"Yes, well." She eyed him up and down. "I think I'll do away with the speech and put you out of your misery forthright. You have no desire whatsoever to marry me, do you?"

Alphonse startled, desperate to have someone other than Jacobi who might understand his plight, but he caught himself in the nick of time and looked around, hurriedly, as if his mother might be hidden in one of the nearby rosebushes to catch him in the act.

Aaliyah laughed. "It's quite alright. You're perfectly obvious about it: you wear your heart on your sleeve. It's why I chose you."

"I really don't—"

"I remember you from that party last summer. Your mother was rather keen to sic me on you then, as well. You were wonderfully oblivious to it all."

"Miss Aaliyah—"

"Hush," she said, and guided him to a little bench that was half engulfed by a flowering snowball bush.

Sitting, they angled in towards each other, their knees not quite brushing, and she caught his hands earnestly between her own. His heart in his mouth, fluttering with all the panic of a wounded bird, he hushed.

"I agreed to play along with your mother's plans precisely because I knew about your lack of interest in me."

"Oh?" he managed.

"What I need is less a husband and more a sympathetic partner, and I believe you and I aren't as different as we might appear."

"Are we not?" he asked doubtfully.

"I don't want a husband any more than you want a wife, but our families insist on it."

For the first time all week, hope sprang in his breast. "You've got fortitude and intelligence and all that in your corner, though. One of those steel cores they're always going on about. Me, I'll roll over and do what they tell me, but you don't seem the sort to go down without a fight. Even if your family disinherited you, I imagine you'd do just fine for yourself, what?"

"I considered it, but sometimes, the best path really is the one of least resistance. I mean to have my cake and eat it, too, and I'm offering you the chance for the same. So, Alphonse: even if you don't want me as a wife, would you have me as a friend and confidante?"

Alphonse thawed. "I've always been of the mind that one can never have too many friends," he said, hesitantly.

"Excellent." She flashed him a smile and squeezed his hands. "Then you really ought to propose to me right now, before it gets too dark for them to see us."

"Now, wait a minute—"

"If you think they're not spying on us through the windows—"

"Of course they're spying on us, but I thought you were on my side! We just agreed that we didn't want to be married!"

"I am on your side. Once we have a little more breathing room I'll be able to explain everything, and I hope we'll come to a comfortable arrangement for the both of us. But until then, I really don't see any way out of this but through."

Alphonse opened and shut his mouth a few times in succession, like an ineffective goldfish.

"Oh, come on."

Still clasping his hands, she guided him off the bench and onto the ground at her feet, where he knelt, feeling as though he had lost track of the conversation some time ago, and it had gone cheerfully on without him while he sat derailed in its wake, wondering when he had fallen off.

"Propose," she ordered.

"I haven't even got a ring!"

"We'll sort that out later."

Seeing that she was unmovable, Alphonse assumed the position, one knee pressed to the dewy ground. Aaliyah offered him her hand, which he took, though he wasn't entirely sure what to do with it. For lack of a better idea, he folded it between the both of his, and hoped it looked chivalric to anyone watching from the dining room.

"Er," he said, beginning on a strong note, and then clearing his throat. "Miss Aaliyah Kaddour. Though we've only just met, and I must admit to being terribly befuddled as to how this whole thing has happened, I can't imagine a better wife than you. Therefore, will you do me the great honour of marrying me?"

"Oh, Alphonse. I thought you'd never ask." She rose with an amused little smile and drew him to his feet. When they were both upright, she leaned in with one hand on his chest to press a sweet kiss to his cheek. "Listen," she said, in a low voice directly into his ear. "If it turns out that we're just terrible together and we can't stand each other's company, we'll call the whole thing off. I'll manage it so that your mother can't possibly blame you. Alright?"

"Alright," he conceded, still utterly dumbfounded. "It's a plan. Of some sort."

"Here." She made an elegant gesture with her hands, and a burst of magic sparked from her fingertips, shimmering into an oblong figure that was almost as tall as she was. It shaped itself into an armful of long flower stalks, which she held between them with a smile. "Since we haven't a ring, yet," she explained.

The pastel flowers were fat and bell-shaped, hanging off the stalks and bobbing cheerfully with her every movement.

"They're lovely," he said admiringly. "What are they?"

"Hollyhocks, silly."

He reached out one hand to touch the petals, and they exploded in a shower of pale drops. She drew back to smile at him, and there, surrounded by the ponderous snowball blossoms and so many dusky roses with their gentle perfume, she really did look like the loveliest creature in all the world.

His fiancée.

Oh, merciful god. What had he got himself into?

♦ ♦ ♦

After that, they had to announce their engagement to the rest of the dinner party, who all pretended as if it were a total surprise, and then they had to accept their congratulatory drinks and numerous rounds of well wishes, so that it wasn't until after one in the morning that Alphonse was finally able to beg exhaustion and excuse himself from the whole sordid affair. His mother only allowed his escape because he had, after all, followed her instructions to a tee, and bade him good night with the promise (or threat) to see him again shortly, to arrange the wedding. He bid Aaliyah good night and good bye with a perfunctory kiss to the cheek, gratified to note that she, too, was looking somewhat overwhelmed by that point, and then all but collapsed into Jacobi's arms the moment they were out of sight.

"Take me home, Jacobi," he moaned, listing into the man's side as they walked to the car. "I'm not sure I forgive you for abandoning me to my fate like that, but I shall have to sort it out in the morning, because I'm entirely deceased."

"You've seen later nights than this at the Stag's Head, surely, sir."

"That may well be, but the Stag's Head has never beset me with fiancées."

Jacobi opened the passenger side door for him, waiting passively for him to shuffle his poor body inside. Though Alphonse half expected to fall asleep on the drive back to the city, he couldn't quiet his mind, and it buzzed away like a hornet until Jacobi pulled into the Portman Square garage.

"A soothing tea before bed, sir?" Jacobi asked, as they rode the lift. "You have had a trying day, if I may say so."

"Yes, that might help."

"Might I offer a sleeping aid with it?"

"Something to put me out of my misery, what?"

Once in the flat, with Jacobi vanishing to the kitchen to put the kettle on, Alphonse shed his suit for his pyjamas and slipped between the bedcovers, his thoughts scattered. He so rarely had more than one at a time that he had little practice putting them back in order, and found that the process hurt his head. How brainy chaps like Jacobi did it on the regular, he had no idea.

Jacobi shimmered in with a chamomile tea and a plate of perfectly golden toast, dripping butter. "Will there be anything else, sir?"

"Do you think I did the right thing? She was talking about how I should look at her as an ally rather than a fiancée, but I hardly know what that means. She's up to something more nefarious than getting engaged, but I haven't the foggiest what I'm supposed to do with that information."

"I can't say anything for certain, sir, but her words do suggest that she is on the same page as you regarding the institute of marriage."

"What page is that?" Alphonse asked blankly.

"That you are both disinterested in the opposite sex as anything more than friendly company, sir," Jacobi replied, patiently.

Alphonse chewed on that for a moment. "Because I'm not interested in her—intimately, that is—she thinks I'm a safe bet for going along with whatever plan she's hatching?"

"It's very possible, sir."

"So, she mightn't expect me to perform any husbandly duties during our marriage?" he clarified, his hopes brightening.

"From what I've gathered, that does seem a likely outcome, sir."

"Then this could turn out to be a sort of sham marriage, what? Perfectly respectable and mother-proof on the surface, but in private, we might retire to our separate rooms at the end of the day and go about our separate business, and, and keep our separate staff? And things might not have to change so drastically after all?"

"That would be the best-case scenario, sir, yes."

Alphonse took a swig of his tea and found, rather than the expected bitter aftertaste of sleep-inducing chemicals, an uncharacteristic sweetness. He swallowed it down all the same. "Do you think I should go ahead with it?" he finally asked. "I feel like a rabbit caught between the fence and the hounds, and one of them is marriage and the other, my mother, and they're both as likely to tear me to shreds."

"Sir. If I may."

Jacobi approached to stand at the foot of the bed, his hands clasped behind his back. The glow of the lamplight softened his features and burnished him in gold, so that he looked more like an oil painting than the sharp, cutting figure with which Alphonse was familiar.

"You are a good man, sir, and any young woman should be lucky to have you as her spouse. Miss Kaddour is a fine match, and, if I have read her correctly, perhaps the best wife you could wish to find."

"It's not going to be one of those marriages where we gradually grow to love each other," Alphonse warned. "I might like her well enough as a friend, but as a wife? I simply can't imagine myself—"

"That's quite alright, sir. From what you've told me of your inclinations, I would never expect it of you. And nor, I think, would Miss Kaddour."

Alphonse sat back against the pillows, cradling his tea. "Alright, then. As long as everyone's expectations are managed."

"You must try to look at it optimistically, sir."

"I'll have my inheritance," Alphonse owned, trying to bolster his spirits.

"Indeed, sir. Is there anything else I can do for you this evening?"

"No, no. I think I might sit up a while longer, just, you know. Pondering the state of things, as one does." He stifled an enormous yawn.

"As you wish, sir. Will you finish your tea and toast, or shall I take them away?"

"I'll finish them." Alphonse took another drink, then wrinkled his nose, trying to identify that taste. "I say, did you add sugar to this, Jacobi?"

"Is it unpleasant, sir?"

"No, not at all, just dashed unexpected, like. I can't place the flavour. You said it was chamomile?"

"Yes, sir. With an added sleeping aid, as we discussed."

Alphonse sniffed the tea, but couldn't make out anything druggy in it. It smelled fruity, almost, like the whiff of summer magic. "It doesn't taste like any sleeping aid I've had before, is all."

THE BACHELOR'S VALET

"I like to keep a modest collection of natural remedies at hand, sir," Jacobi said neutrally, "in the event that the young master takes ill, for example, and can't stomach the stronger chemical doses."

"Good thinking. Brains like yours never fail to be prepared." Alphonse swallowed down the rest of the mug, and, sure enough, began to feel his eyelids droop mere moments later. Crunching his way through his toast, he made short work of it before passing the dishes off to Jacobi, who collected them with a wordless bow.

"Perhaps I'll leave the ponderings of the universe to another night," Alphonse said around another mighty yawn. "Dashed powerful stuff, that, isn't it? Whatever it is, keep it stocked, will you?"

"Gladly, sir."

"Good night, Jacobi," Alphonse said blearily, blindly dropping to his pillow, eyes already shut.

He heard Jacobi turn off the lamp, the glow behind his eyelids blinking out and giving way to the fuzzy dark of the wee hours.

"Sleep well, sir."

Alphonse burrowed beneath the covers, every misgiving melting away beneath the heavy sensation of sleep, and his last thought was that the tea really had smelled like magic, but he dropped off before he could work out what that meant.

♦ ♦ ♦

The cottage took form all around him as he lay on his back gazing up at the stars. He watched with hazy interest as it solidified, constellations winking down at him from between the rafters until the ceiling filled in all the gaps and he was blinking up at the pots and pans hanging from the kitchen beams. Gradually, he realised that he wasn't on the ground at all, but sprawled low in a plush armchair in front of the kitchen fireplace. The fire was barely burning, just a warm glow emanating from the embers. Alphonse gave a mighty stretch, his arms all the way over his head and his toes pointed to the hearth, relishing the movement. His body was sluggish, like his limbs were all weighed down, but it didn't seem like the dreams where he was trapped in slow-motion like an ant in honey, so he didn't give it much mind. Jacobi was comfortably ensconced in the chair beside him, and Alphonse was confident that Jacobi could rescue him from any unpleasantness if the need arose. Snug in Jacobi's lap with a book propped up against her was the tabby cat, while a cup of tea balanced on the arm of the chair and a pair of thin-framed glasses perched on Jacobi's aquiline nose.

Alphonse had never seen him wear glasses before. Did he wear them after hours, or was it a mere figment of Alphonse's imagination? Perhaps they were only for reading. In any case, they suited him. Jacobi had always seemed wise beyond his years, but the glasses lent him a distinguished look, to say nothing of how they enhanced the cut of his cheekbones. He looked like he should be a professor or an historian or some such brainy fellow, tucked away in a stately university or museum office, surrounded by heaps of important books. Possibly books that he himself had authored. Or standing at a podium giving a lecture to all manner of likewise intelligent chaps, all of whom would listen with baited breath to receive his genius.

Jacobi glanced over, letting his book fall closed as he kept his place with one thumb between the pages. "You're quiet tonight."

"I was just thinking how lucky I am to have this. Here, now, with you. I don't appreciate you enough, old chap. Or rather, I don't tell you often enough just how much I appreciate you. I mean, I do try. But you always shut me down before I can get the proper words out. I suppose it is inappropriate, a bit, letting me gush on about you, but, well. You deserve the praise, man. All that and more."

"I feel appreciated," Jacobi said, setting his book aside for good as amusement coloured his words. "If I didn't, I wouldn't have stayed nearly as long as I have. I do have some sense of self-worth, you know."

"You don't get tired of me?" Alphonse asked, tipping his head back against the chair to stare up at the ceiling. If he looked through his eyelashes, he could just see the stars poking their heads through the rafters, like the roof had never covered them at all. "Picking up after my messes and shepherding me to and fro and putting up with all my nonsense? I must be exhausting."

"I rather enjoy your nonsense, as a matter of fact."

Jacobi stroked one hand over the cat's back and was rewarded with a sleepy purr. His fingers sank into the plush fur, and Alphonse stared, mesmerised by their simple elegance. Had he ever noticed Jacobi's hands before? They were always there; surely he must have. But seeing them now, broad-backed and long-fingered, the nails as neatly manicured as his own, though somehow so much more capable—

"Alphonse."

Alphonse startled from his reverie, blinking at Jacobi with what he was sure was an amazed expression. He had never heard his name in Jacobi's mouth before, not in all their years together, and it warmed him to his core, making him go all bubbly inside, like a bottle of champagne about to burst. Jacobi looked back at him, faint concern etching the tiniest groove in between his eyebrows. Alphonse wanted to press the pad of his thumb to the mark to erase it, like smudging away an ink blot.

"Are you alright?" Jacobi asked, one hand on the side of his chair like he meant to reach over and touch Alphonse's arm. Like that was something they did. Like it was something he wanted to do.

"Oh," said Alphonse stupidly.

Jacobi's hand was ever so slightly darker than his own, with a thin scar along the base of the thumb where Jacobi had burned himself with the iron one day early in his employ. It had been Alphonse's fault, blundering into the man while blathering away at some inane one-sided conversation without paying attention to where he was walking. The burn had healed into something shiny and white, and Alphonse wanted to touch it, suddenly, to see if it felt as glossy as it looked, and to apologise all over again, even though Jacobi had forgiven him years ago.

"Jacobi," he began, not knowing what he was going to say next. He felt on the verge of some momentous realisation, positively giddy with it, and just as soon as he could pinpoint what that realisation was, he was going to tell Jacobi all about it. He had never been all that good with words, but if he could just articulate this one thing—

He blinked and the world swam before his eyes like he was underwater. The cottage shimmered, the fireplace wavering, and he held out one hand to steady himself, but it only served to disorient him further. His fingers were long and wobbly, like he was looking at them submerged in invisible water, and he lost time moving them back and forth, the dull firelight refracting around his skin.

"Dashed powerful stuff," he repeated, vaguely.

"Alphonse," Jacobi said again.

Alphonse pulled his attention back. Jacobi wore an expression that suggested he had been saying Alphonse's name for some time, and Alphonse regretted having missed it. "Sorry, old thing. I've clean forgot was I was going to say. My head's not in the right place at all, I'm afraid." He cracked a yawn, smothering it with one hand. "Sorry, sorry. I think I'd better get some proper rest, what? I'll just head back outside to where I was before, under the stars and whatnot, and see if that clears things up." He rose from his chair, unsteady on his legs, and gave Jacobi a pat on the shoulder. Jacobi bled heat through his suit, and

Alphonse left his hand there for a second longer than he planned, soaking it up as surely as that cat in Jacobi's lap was soaking up the same. "If I ever remember what it was I meant to tell you, I'll come straight back in," he promised.

"Alright," Jacobi said, though concern still marked his brow. Fainter now, but the urge to smooth it away was still there.

Alphonse weaved his way through the kitchen to the door with its little four-square panel of glass, but before he could go through it, Jacobi said, "Here, take this with you. For company."

One of those little light orbs sparked out from between Jacobi's thumb and forefinger, wavering in the air like a firefly for a second before growing larger and more ponderous, and bobbing its way to Alphonse's side.

"Oh, hullo," Alphonse said to it, holding out one hand. It lit down on his fingertip like a butterfly, nearly weightless, and a delightful shimmery feeling rushed through him.

When he looked up, Jacobi was watching him with an expression of awful fondness, a smile curling in the corners of his mouth like a secret just between the two of them. And Alphonse wanted to press his fingers there, too, and trace his lips and eyelids and the strong slope of his nose, except he felt so awfully heavy, and his mind was filling up with cotton batting that prevented him from saying any of that out loud, much less crossing the little kitchen to act on it. As his tongue grew thicker and woollen, the cottage dissolved around him like mist, and he floated out into space like a dust mote, the soft little orb of light at his side.

He stayed like that for some interminable time, swimming in the deep subconscious soup of sleep, until the cycle shifted and he found himself in his car trying to navigate downtown London streets that were flooded with water up past the wheels. It sloshed around inside the cab, cold but not necessarily unpleasant, and it wouldn't have been so bad at all if it weren't for the fish. A fat, shiny salmon stared up at him mournfully from around his feet, and a fleet of mackerel flickered around the gear stick. The fish didn't want to be there any more than he wanted them around, but when he tried to roll the windows down to give them a means of escape, more fish flopped their way inside. It was with mounting frustration that he steered his car along, looking for wherever he was supposed to be going—and he'd be damned if he could remember, but it was awfully important that he wasn't late—but the fish outside kept getting bigger and blocking his view of things.

When he finally woke in his bed, he dragged one hand through his hair with a put-upon groan.

"Blasted fish dream again," he muttered.

It was always the fish dream, in times of stress. He vaguely remembered an earlier dream, something far more pleasant than the fish—something involving Jacobi?—but of course his brain could only conjure up the mackerel. Flopping onto his back, he turned his head to the side to gaze at the sliver of light edging around the curtains, his brow crumpled as he worked to remember. He had only fleeting images to cling to: Jacobi's face lit up by dim firelight, stars winking down from in between ceiling beams, and the soft glow of magic. Mostly, he was left with a warm sense of comfort and genuine companionship, heating him up from the inside like a good drink. It felt like home, is what it felt like.

"Only right that Jacobi should be there, then," Alphonse sleepily informed the curtains.

But there was something else about the dream, too, something that made him feel bubbly and excited, like he had a secret he needed to share. If he could just pinpoint that feeling and put a name to it, everything in his life would become clear, like fog wisping away to reveal a bright summer sky. But he'd always been rubbish at identifying feelings, and the longer he stayed awake noodling at it, the fainter the dream became, so eventually he gave up and shut his eyes, succumbing to the last remnants of the drug in his system.

CHAPTER FOUR

A CONVERSATION IN THE WATERLILY HOUSE OF KEW GARDENS

Alphonse took the weekend to recover from the shock of his engagement. Jacobi patiently coached him through it, reassuring him at every turn, until Alphonse finally exhausted himself of arguments and theories. He was to be married, and there was no telling what that marriage would be like until he was in it. It seemed an unreasonable way to live, but there was no more to be done.

With that rather nihilistic mindset, he answered the telephone on Monday morning with a dreary "Hullo," that was as a far cry from his normally chipper greeting.

"Come to Kew Gardens," Aaliyah said, without preamble.

Alphonse blinked. "Now? Today?"

"The sooner the better, with your mother pushing for the wedding like she is. I thought it was time we laid our cards on the table, before it's too late to call the whole thing off."

"When you put it like that—"

"One o' clock?" she suggested.

"I—well, yes, alright. I'll be there."

"Excellent. I'll see you then." And with no further fanfare, she hung up, leaving Alphonse staring at the silent receiver.

"She's quite the abrupt thing, isn't she? She was so polite at dinner for my mother, but the instant it's one on one, she drops all that to get straight to the point."

"I imagine Miss Kaddour is a woman of many layers, sir."

"Do you think it's due to her family's business sense? That no-nonsense approach?"

"I'm sure it plays a part, sir."

"Hm." Alphonse dropped the receiver back in its cradle. "I suppose there are worse things than to marry into a family of entrepreneurs."

"To be sure, sir. As I said before, she seems like a good match for you."

"My mother certainly thinks so. Presumably because she recognised a fellow female of the species keen on bossing me around."

"Don't despair, sir. I expect this meeting will unveil the answers to all your reservations. Besides which, I was of the impression that you thrived in a more controlled environment."

"Excuse me, but I am very much a master of my own destiny, Jacobi!"

"Yes, sir."

"The captain of my own soul!"

"Indubitably, sir."

Alphonse huffed. "Good. Now, what am I supposed to wear to this thing?"

Jacobi's mouth tilted upwards. "Allow me to peruse your wardrobe and make a selection."

♦ ♦ ♦

Alphonse arrived at Kew in a suit of robin's-egg blue and a state of panic, already five minutes late, despite Jacobi's best efforts.

"I should have got her a ring," he said wildly. "I can't turn up empty handed the first time meeting post-engagement, even if it is all contrived. It just doesn't seem right."

"It's a little late for a ring now, sir."

"Do you think she's noticed I'm late? I'll just find one of those flower-sellers and grab her something quick. Go stall for time until I get there!"

Alphonse then flung himself from the car in the direction of the nearest flower vendor while Jacobi suffered a discreet sigh, straightened his suit, and strode off to find his young master's fiancée. Alphonse cast glances over his shoulder at his man the whole time he was talking to the vendor, who seemed amused by his struggles. After another two minutes, Alphonse left the vendor with an enormous, magic-crafted bouquet of pastel things, nearly tripping over his own feet as he hastened to catch up with his valet.

As it turned out, he needn't have hurried quite so much, as Jacobi and Aaliyah seemed perfectly content in polite conversation—that was to say, Jacobi, Aaliyah, and an unknown third party in the form of a young black woman. She wore a bright floral dress under a coat and a cloche hat, and leaned in to whisper in Aaliyah's ear when she spoke, too softly for the words to carry. Aaliyah had a glimmering shawl draped around her shoulders, and a few loose strands of her hair had escaped her careful waves to drift in the autumn breeze. Her dress was dark red, matching her lips, and decorated with those art-nouveau-style panels designed to make her torso look even longer and slimmer than it already was. Her coat was long, and so brown it was almost black. The three of them looked awfully striking together crowded around the greenhouse entrance, the girls bright as jewels, and Jacobi all in black like a shadow, svelte and attentive.

Alphonse stumbled to a halt some yards away, struck by the image. He was so used to having Jacobi glued to his side that he rarely saw him from a distance, much less in the company of others, and found he rather appreciated the sight. It was hard to notice how tall Jacobi was when he was right beside him all the time, and for all that Alphonse was used to the man blending into the background, as unobtrusive as any good valet should be, he really stood out like a sore thumb, stark against the shimmering green of the glass. His hair sleeked back just so, his eyelashes like dark smudges against his cheeks as he leaned in, head inclined to catch what the girls were saying. A cutting figure like a work of art that should be in magazines or galleries, or out on the dance floor. Somewhere to be admired and respected, not tucked away in the servant's quarters.

Alphonse had been stood staring too long. Jacobi glanced his way, a question in his eyes, though he didn't do anything to draw attention to the fact that Alphonse was frozen in place just beyond them. Still, Aaliyah was a sharp thing, and she caught sight of him the instant Jacobi did.

"There you are! Your man said you were delayed. Are you ready to join us?"

"Quite," he stammered, and picked his way over the path to them. "Terribly sorry to keep you waiting, though now I feel like I'm interrupting. Shall I let you three continue your conversation, and I'll just…?"

"Don't be silly," Aaliyah said briskly, though she tempered it with a smile. "We were just passing the time, and Miss Bailey's not staying in any case."

The black girl nodded Alphonse a greeting, or perhaps a good bye. "But it's nice to meet you, however briefly, Mr. Hollyhock."

"And you," he replied automatically. "Er, Jacobi—"

"I thought I might accompany Miss Bailey to her next appointment while you and Miss Kaddour discuss matters, sir," Jacobi said pleasantly, "and meet you back at the car when you're finished, if that's agreeable."

Alphonse looked at Jacobi and Miss Bailey together. They made a striking pair, with her bright fashion next to his stylish black, and though his stomach flipped uncomfortably for reasons he couldn't articulate to think of them together like *that*, who was he to stand in their way?

"That's certainly a better way to spend your time than waiting for me in the car," he said with forced levity that caused Jacobi to look at him askance. "You two enjoy the day, and Aaliyah and I shall strive to do the same."

"It will be a trial, I'm sure," Aaliyah said drily. "I'll see you two around."

Jacobi offered Miss Bailey his arm, as gallant as any gentleman, and the two of them disappeared around the side of the greenhouse and into the garden proper. Alphonse watched them go with no small amount of dread, but once they were out of sight, he could no longer put off the inevitable and turned back to Aaliyah with a bilious smile.

"You're looking well," she said, as if nothing was amiss. "Are those for me?"

He handed her the bouquet, which she had to accept with both arms, before leaning in to press an awkward kiss to her cheek.

"Hollyhocks again, you see? Ha."

"Thank you, they're beautiful." She tucked them in the crook of one arm to lay against her shoulder, like a soldier hoisting a rifle.

Alphonse slung his hands in his pockets with no idea how to proceed. "I haven't got a ring for you yet. I don't know what style you like, and I thought, since we're meeting each other halfway in this, that you ought to have some say in the design, what?"

"That's very thoughtful of you."

"I suppose we'll have to get that sorted sooner than later," he blathered on. "Wouldn't do to turn up at our own wedding without an engagement ring, eh? Or wedding rings, either."

"Alphonse."

"Have you got preferences about weddings?" he asked, increasingly desperate to latch onto some form of conversation. "I'm told most women do. I imagine you'll want to plan out dresses and centrepieces and, and flowers, and whatnot. Or perhaps Mother will take care of all that. Or the both of you together? Though that seems a cruel and unusual punishment, doesn't it, forcing Mother's company on you—"

"Alphonse."

He snapped his trap shut.

"You've never gone out with a girl before, have you?"

"Socially, yes, but they're usually cousins. Or, or whatever girls the chaps are seeing at the time. Not, er, in the romantic sense of the word, no."

She smiled in a way that seemed designed to set him at ease, and which therefore only made him all the more nervous. Years of growing up under his mother's thumb had taught him to never trust a feminine smile.

"Then let's pretend I'm one of those other girls, shall we? Already spoken for, or otherwise unavailable." She lowered her gaze, a line of tension creasing her brow. "I had hoped we could go into this as friends. I don't want you to make things awkward, playing at romantic gestures when we both know that neither of us want any such thing."

"I didn't mean…"

"I thought we had an understanding, Alphonse. Our lack of interest in one another: indeed, in the opposite sex at all. I don't want you to court me, not now that we're already engaged."

"You're right," he managed. "I just panic, you see, and I still don't have a clear picture of your motives, no matter how Jacobi tries to reassure me. So, I thought I ought to try to do things right, with the flowers and whatnot. Because you are my fiancée, even if I don't know why." He glanced around. A few other couples drifted by, weaving in and out of the sprawling flower beds, following the little winding paths that led around the massive, glittering structure of the greenhouse. "Also, I can never be sure when Mother is watching, and I don't want her accusing me of bunging the whole thing up."

Aaliyah relaxed, her fingers curling delicately around the stems of the bouquet. "I understand. And I'll add my reassurances to your man's that you have nothing to fear in this marriage. In fact, let's go inside, somewhere more private, and then I can put a stop to your worries once and for all."

"Awfully secretive, what?"

"It's not something I want to discuss in public, and neither do you."

"Righto. Lead the way, then, and I'll follow."

THE BACHELOR'S VALET

She took his arm and looped it through the one of hers that wasn't taken up by a bunch of flowers, and marched them through the swooping doors of the greenhouse. Stepping inside, they were immediately swamped with thick, buffeting humidity. A jungle of greenery and bright bobbing flowers sprang up a mere yard within the entrance. Kew Gardens had grown exponentially since Princess Augusta founded the place back in the 1700s, the main greenhouse building ever upward and outward with new rooms and pathways added by the year, turning the once modest acreage into a veritable city of glasshouses. If Alphonse were forced to partake in nature he preferred the wide romping fields of a hunting course, or perhaps the pond at the back of the Hollyhock estate where he had dabbled as a boy, but he dutifully acknowledged the splendour of the Royal Botanic Gardens all the same. The flora was obviously well cared for, even if he didn't know how to properly appreciate it.

Aaliyah made small-talk as she led him along the paths, the sort of light mindless chatter that played to Alphonse's strengths. She pointed out plants and flowers as they passed, or commented on passers-by's fashion, or remarked on how clever the magic system was to keep the climate so carefully controlled. In short, she behaved just as she had done at the dinner party, which was to say, masked in falsehoods. Now that Alphonse knew her true nature—a brusque, devious one—he couldn't trust anything she said, no matter how pleasant or innocuous.

"These ones are native to North Africa," she told him, pointing to a cluster of small plants with sharp red leaves and bursts of tiny yellow flowers. "We call them God's Tongue. Father always keeps one in the garden for medicinal use."

"They're pretty things." Alphonse leaned in to give them a good look. "They've got a sharp smell to them, what? Like spices."

"Don't get too close. The smell alone can have a powerful effect."

He scooted back. "You don't say?"

"They're used as pain relief in Algeria, but they can come on awfully strong for someone not used to them."

"Is that so? Sounds like jolly good fun."

"It is, until you realise you've been laying on the floor studying carpet patterns for the past four hours. Come on."

She led him through an arched glass corridor lined with great stripy plants that grew waist-high and were painted in swaths of red and yellow and fuchsia on top of their dark greens, like girls in bright party dresses, and into the Waterlily House.

The Waterlily House was a small square glasshouse with vines climbing the ceiling structure, from which hung every size and shape of gourd imaginable, all decked out in their fall-time colours. Alphonse craned his neck to gawp at them as Aaliyah steered him inside.

"Say, they're not at risk of dropping down and braining a chap, are they?"

"Not for another week or two," Aaliyah assured him, tugging him down to sit beside her on a little bench overlooking the pond.

The pond spanned nearly the whole width of the glasshouse, a great circular thing filled with glossy black water, with lush greenery brimming at the edges, and its centre filled with flowering lily pads. Most were the little flat ones he was used to seeing, but some were enormous, large enough for a full-grown man to sit on, with their edges upturned like a little wall all around the outside, as if the pads were intending to grow entire civilizations on their surface. Little dots of light bopped lazily from the ceiling to the water and back again, some no larger than a firefly, and some the span of his palm, all glowing with warm, fuzzy light. The sight of them filled him with an overpowering sense of déjà vu, so strong he had to blink to dispel the notion that he ought to be sitting in a humble cottage garden rather than the shiny magnificence that was Kew.

"Well, that's something, isn't it?"

"They're purely decorative," Aaliyah said, and, with a careless wave of her fingers, sent one of her own little light-orbs off to join the others.

"I wish I could do that," Alphonse said admiringly.

Light tricks didn't take any effort at all, or so he'd been led to believe, but even the simplest of magical endeavours were beyond him. When he waggled his fingers like that, he didn't get anything to show for it but judgemental stares.

"I'll do you one better," Aaliyah said, and drew an unrecognisable pattern in the air with one fingertip.

Something rippled out from the centre point like the sheen on the skin of a soap bubble, engulfing the two of them where they sat, before dissipating. "A privacy screen," Aaliyah explained. "Whatever we talk about in here won't be overheard, no matter who comes wandering by."

"Won't anyone think it strange, seeing us sitting here with our mouths flapping but no sound coming out?"

"They'll hear it as some language they don't know. Now, let's get down to business." Setting her bundle of hollyhocks on the bench between them, she turned to face Alphonse with a determined air. "I'll be frank. Neither of us particularly wants to be married to the other, but I think we can make this work. You see, I'm in love with someone already, to whom marriage is utterly impossible. My father is progressive in most ways, but, for the sake of continuing the family business, he still insists that I marry someone of a suitable class and sex. That is to say: wealthy and male. Which is where you enter the picture, pressured for similar reasons, I assume. Minus the family business."

"Quite," he said faintly.

"So, here is my proposal: we give them exactly what they want. We marry, have a grand old wedding and put on a show of everything being shiny and bright and just what they asked for, and in private, we go about our usual lives without anything having changed, except for living together. What do you say?"

"When you say without anything having changed…"

"I keep my lover, and you keep your man," Aaliyah replied promptly. "We'll have to move from your flat into a proper house, of course. We'll need the privacy, not to mention the space, but we'll keep separate bedrooms, which is common enough. No outside staff; it's much too difficult to vet people like that."

"I see." Alphonse swallowed. "And as far as the wedding night goes…"

"There won't be one," she said, in a tone that brooked no compromise. "No marriage bed, wedding night, nor wifely duties."

"Nor husbandly," he added, hope springing in his chest once more.

"No, nor husbandly. I want nothing more from you than the appearance of a loving marriage, a friendly peck on the cheek when the occasion calls for it, and the necessary kiss at the altar itself. We shall be as intimate as two people living together must be, but no more. And then, after a few years of seeming marital bliss, we'll regretfully inform our families that I cannot get with child. By that time, it will be far too awkward for them to do anything but carry on, and that will be that." She folded her hands on her knees and waited for his response.

Alphonse blew out his breath in a gusty sigh of relief. "I must say, that does take a weight off my mind."

"I'm glad to hear it."

"You seem to have thought it all through. So, we're to be married on paper, and in private we're more like…housemates?"

"Precisely, yes."

"And no one will raise questions about your lover living with us?"

"No more than they would question you keeping your valet," she said, looking pleased. "If anyone asks, she's my personal assistant and I can't bear to part with her. No one would expect me to step into my father's role of managing the company without a trusted personal assistant."

"Oh, she's a *she*," Alphonse said stupidly.

Aaliyah studied him for a moment. "I assumed that wouldn't be a problem, especially not for someone like you. Was I wrong, Mr. Hollyhock?"

"Not at all! I only thought— Well, I didn't think at all, frankly, and I'm sorry for it. Didn't mean to offend."

He dropped into silence for a moment, trying to puzzle out how exactly two women were meant to get on in that way. Two men was straightforward enough, and of course a man and a woman could do it easily… A voice in his head that sounded suspiciously like Jacobi warned him not to say any of that out loud.

He cleared his throat. "Hang on, though: what do you mean, someone like me?"

"Someone of your persuasion. Or rather, our persuasion."

"Er?"

"You and Jacobi."

He waited expectantly for her to follow that up with something else. Instead, she merely looked at him like he was meant to have followed along. People often gave him such looks early in their acquaintance, until they figured out that he rarely followed anything but the simplest and most straightforward track.

"You do like men, don't you?"

"Oh, yes! I've only recently learned that was an option, but apparently yes, I do. Jacobi was the one who told me so, in fact. But what else has he got to do with this?"

She stared at him. He blinked back at her.

"Well, perhaps we'll revisit this conversation at a future date," she finally said.

"Right," he said, relieved at not being asked to do any further noodling. "As for the rest of it— You know, I've never lived with anyone besides Jacobi. Well, and Mother, but one shouldn't count that."

"I'm sure you'll take it in stride. Until then, I suggest we become friends. How do you socialize with your cousins and your friends' fiancées? Treat me as you would them, and we'll get along just splendidly. Better yet, treat me as you would one of the boys. I rather like the thought of that." She flashed him a bright smile, and he couldn't help but be charmed by it.

"Very well. In that case, I should invite you to the hunt this weekend, at the Featherstrop estate. Do you ride?"

"I most certainly do. Let's call it a date."

She reached over to squeeze his hand, and for the first time, Alphonse didn't feel a flare of panic in response, but rather the excitement of having found a co-conspirator.

CHAPTER FIVE

WHEREIN ALPHONSE FALLS OFF A HORSE AND INTO A HEDGE

The Featherstrop estate was every bit as unnecessarily large as the Hollyhock one, and a ripping place for a fox hunt. Alphonse had never been particularly keen on hunting, partially because he had an unfortunate habit of getting his horse tangled up in the hounds, but also because he could never quite shake the feeling of sympathy for the poor beast. That said, he did enjoy the bright, noisy chaos of it all: the baying of the hounds and the racket of thundering hooves over the green, and the joyful shouts of his fellows all clamouring for attention. There was an easy camaraderie to hunting. He'd known most of the chaps since they were schoolboys, and there was much jostling of knees and elbows amongst one another as they went riding all-out over the bright hilly landscape of the countryside. The treetops rippled in the autumn breeze, and the sun was a dazzlingly white ball of fire in the clear blue sky. The air was the sharp, clear kind that filled the head with the scent of frost-tipped grass, strong enough to make the mouth water.

Aaliyah had accepted Alphonse's offer to drive up together, and turned up at Portman Square wearing a smart tweed riding jacket, breeches and knee-high boots, all set off with a cap perched on her head at a jaunty angle, and she looked so boyish that she short-circuited Alphonse's brain for a second before he put everything back in order. If she had turned up to the dinner party looking like that, he might have gone along with his mother's engagement plan a little more readily. But no: that was his confusion talking. Dumbstruck, he allowed Jacobi to shepherd them both into the backseat of the car.

"You look good," he managed. "I mean, you look well."

"Thank you." She glanced at him sideways, an amused slant to her mouth. "Is it the trousers throwing you off?"

"Somewhat," he confessed. "But you did say you wanted to be treated as one of the lads, so I shouldn't be too surprised. You make an awfully good-looking chap, is all. Rather caught me off guard."

Reaching over, she gave him a firm pat on the knee. "Don't fret, Alphonse. You're not attracted to me. It's just the suit."

"Oh, thank god. I was worried I was going to make things terribly awkward."

"Sir? Why don't you tell Miss Kaddour about your friends she's to meet?" Jacobi politely interjected from the front seat, saving Alphonse from embarrassing himself further.

This was the first time he had ever brought a friend along to a hunt, and most certainly the first time he had ever brought a friend of the feminine persuasion. Still, Featherstrop had put it about that all the chaps ought to bring their girls along, to make a proper party of it, so by the time Alphonse arrived with Aaliyah on his arm—or perhaps he was on hers—the place was absolutely swimming with bright faces and abuzz with cheerful introductions.

Aaliyah made short work of charming his friends, just as she had made short work of charming his family, and was soon firmly encircled by admirers. It should have given Alphonse cause for jealousy, but instead, he found himself relieved.

"Hollyhock! This must be your fiancée!" Featherstrop crowed, making his way over to take Aaliyah's hand and press a kiss to her knuckles. "Darius Featherstrop. So glad you could make it. It's about time he settled down, eh?"

"Aaliyah Kaddour. A pleasure to meet you." She smiled as she retrieved her hand from his grasp.

THE BACHELOR'S VALET

Aaliyah might be immune to Featherstrop's charms and good looks, but Alphonse's knees weakened and his spine went all warm and watery just as they'd done in school whenever Featherstrop had caught his eye. Aaliyah noticed his reaction immediately, of course, and cast him a concerned look from the corner of her eye without dropping her smile. Damn it all, and he'd thought he'd been past all this! He cast around for some excuse to get away.

"Alphonse says that you're old friends," Aaliyah was saying. "You must tell me all about him."

"Oh, you should have met him in his university days! You'd never have got engaged if you'd known him then. He was a right disaster. Weren't you, old chap?"

"I never told your girl any of your embarrassing school day stories," Alphonse replied indignantly. "I dare say she wouldn't have married you, either!"

"Oh, but she met me soon after I graduated. Not like you, trundling on for years after the fact, with no one for company but your valet."

"Let's not bring Jacobi into this."

Featherstrop paused. "No, rather. He's an excellent valet. I do hope you're keeping him after the wedding. What a bother it would be to train a new one."

"I'm afraid it's not really up to me."

Aaliyah glanced between them. "University, then?"

Featherstrop brightened. "Yes! Old Hollyhock here, he'll be the first to tell you that those were his real golden days. I mean, we all had a strapping good time back then, but I dare say that was his peak."

"I wouldn't say that at all!" Alphonse protested. "Why, to suggest that I'd prefer to still be an awkward youth, all coltish legs and, and spots, and whatnot. Simply preposterous."

Featherstrop glanced at him askance. "No, well, not the spots, but other things." He slung his arm around Alphonse's shoulders, reeling him in close and giving him a friendly shake as he turned back to Aaliyah. "I'm glad you're here to take care of the old boy, now. He's been wallowing, I tell you, and I think you're just the thing to snap him out of it."

"Have you been wallowing, Alphonse?"

"I don't think so."

"Wallowing's a strong word," Featherstrop allowed. "But I'm glad you've moved on, in any case. Leaving the trappings of youth behind! Congratulations to the both of you, and what a dashing pair you make, too. Ah, excuse me—I must say hello to Thornbury. Back in a mo!"

He bobbed off and Alphonse let out the breath he'd been holding. He hadn't expected it to be so difficult, coming face to face with Featherstop following their previous conversation. The one in which Alphonse had mortified himself by confessing to his schoolboy infatuation. It had never been so embarrassing in school itself, somehow, when he had actually been in love with the man, but now, years after the fact but with the realisation fresh in his mind, it was absolutely crippling. As Featherstrop sauntered off to greet his other guests, Aaliyah turned to Alphonse with her brows raised, and he felt himself go red at her expression.

"What's that, then?" he asked, feeling that Featherstrop had given something away, though of course he hadn't said anything in particular at all.

"The trappings of youth," she repeated, shaking her head with a smile. "He talks as if you're eighty years old, when I know for a fact you're both firmly in your mid-twenties."

"Ah, yes. He's prided himself on being the first of our lot to get properly engaged—for more than a week, I mean. Quite a show of maturity, he says, and really, who am I to argue?"

"Surely he doesn't expect boys fresh out of university to settle down like that?"

"No, no! Of course not. He's just— Well. There are certain immature acts he'd rather leave behind, what?"

Aaliyah's keen eyes pierced straight through him, and he tugged at his collar, going hot and turning away. Women, with their looks! He's always been right to assume that it wasn't just his mother who could stare into his soul so chillingly.

Before she could interrogate him for details, Featherstrop returned, all smiles and apologies for the interruption. "As I was saying: how a thing like Hollyhock got so lucky, I'll never understand. He had mentioned you earlier, of course, but he never said what a beauty you were. And such exotic looks, too! Tell me, where are you from? Spain, maybe? Or Brazil?"

"Exotic?" Alphonse mouthed to Aaliyah, his nose scrunched up.

"Algeria," Aaliyah said.

"Is that in the Middle East? A very dry, sandy place, I imagine. I expect you're grateful to be able to settle down somewhere more civilised, eh?"

Alphonse didn't have the strongest grasp of geography and might not be able to pinpoint Algeria on a map, but wherever it was, it seemed in bad taste to call anyone's homeland uncivilised. But before he could open his mouth to call Featherstrop out on such a breach of manners, Aaliyah beat him to it, as was right.

"It's in North Africa. And as a matter of fact, I prefer the Maghreb to England, Mr. Featherstrop. I'd prefer it more if it hadn't been brutally colonised by a load of white Europeans, but there you go."

Featherstrop waved one hand, visibly turning away from such a topic. "Ugh, I abhor political talk. It's so terribly dull."

"Of course you think so." Aaliyah rolled her eyes, so dismissive that Alphonse was compelled to clear his throat and step forward to interject.

"Good day for a ride though, what?" he said weakly.

"Oh, yes," Featherstrop agreed, apparently oblivious to Aaliyah's suddenly chilly countenance. "Are you joining us for the hunt proper, Miss Kaddour? Some of the other girls are, and of course we've got horses to spare."

"I should be delighted, Mr. Featherstrop," Aaliyah said, her words clipped and terrifyingly polite. "It's a shame to waste a day like this on small-talk and smaller company."

"Well, we'd best be off to find some horses before all the best ones are spoken for, eh, Aaliyah?" Alphonse said desperately. "Good to see you, Featherstrop! We'll have to do lunch, the four of us—I mean us and Lucy—some time before we're all married off. Or after, I mean, what's the difference, after all? Toodles!"

Taking Aaliyah by the arm, he purposely marched her from the room before she could start a fight with the man. Alphonse was inclined to believe that she would win any fight she set her mind to, but it seemed crass to let such a fight between his fiancée and his old flame happen right under his nose.

The moment they set foot outside, she shook off his hand and said incredulously, "I know it's not on to judge anyone for their school crushes, but really, Alphonse? You're still mooning over that one?"

"I know," he said miserably, trudging towards the stable.

"I can excuse your lovestruck youthfulness for what happened back then; heaven knows I've had an idiotic love affair or two in my time. But now?"

"It was the lack of closure that doomed me. I mean, just look at him! That chiselled jaw! Those muscled thighs! Not to mention his hair or, god, his eyes." Hair in waves like a Roman sculpture, the colour of bright autumn leaves, and copper eyes to match. "He's peak masculinity, is what he is. I'd have to be blind not to appreciate him."

(He was not, in fact, peak anything. A century earlier he'd have been called a fop, but then, so too would have Alphonse.)

"If you were blind, you might realise that he's got absolutely no substance besides his looks," Aaliyah said crossly.

"Neither have I," Alphonse pointed out. "But he's got more brains than I have, and more charm and wit."

"I'm not convinced about his brains, and charm and wit don't necessarily make a man worth knowing. I'd take you over him any day."

"Yes, yes. What with my lack of attraction to the female form, I know."

"Not only that. You're kind, Alphonse, and your heart's in the right place. Men like Featherstrop, they're vapid and self-obsessed. I've met enough to recognise the type at a glance. You deserve better than someone like that. Someone who's not going to dismiss you or take advantage of your good nature, then discard you as soon as they're bored."

"Well," said Alphonse quietly, unable to meet her eye, "it's a shame I only fall for the vapid, self-absorbed ones then, isn't it?"

Aaliyah made a frustrated growl and took him roughly by the arm, startling him into looking up. "And how do you figure Jacobi fits into that, then? Is he vapid and self-absorbed?"

"What? Of course not! He's the epitome of the human race, as far as I'm concerned. The absolute pinnacle."

"And if you'd met him when you were back in school, before you ever met Featherstrop?" she pressed.

"What would a schoolboy need with a valet?" Alphonse asked, baffled.

Aaliyah made a sound of disarticulate rage, rather like a smothered groan, and released him. "Let's go riding," she said decisively, and Alphonse let out a gust of a sigh.

Getting the horses was a welcome change of topic, and the stable was soon bursting with energy as the rest of the hunting party turned up to claim their mounts. Alphonse had an older horse called Lady that he rode every time he visited the estate, a sedate black mare with a white stripe down her nose and an even temperament unbothered by Alphonse's lack of expertise. In contrast, Aaliyah was paired with a spirited young dappled grey mare with a bright-eyed look suggesting that she would be more than happy to throw an inexperienced rider as soon as they set foot to stirrup. Alphonse couldn't have been paid to get on such a horse, but Aaliyah seemed supremely confident as she swung into the saddle, so he left her to it.

"I must tell you straight: I'm hopeless when it comes to fox hunts," he warned her, as they set out into the field along with the rest of the company.

"That's no trouble. I'm not much interested in foxes."

Gathering the reins, she turned her horse out towards the bright green hills. She looked every bit the equestrian in her glossy black boots and her tweed, as at home on horseback as she had been in Kew Gardens, or at the dinner party. Alphonse fumbled his reins in response before deciding it might be best to do as he had always done, and give Lady her head. While Aaliyah's mare was all tossing mane, blowing nostrils and restless hooves, seemingly keen to go tearing off after the hounds just as soon as Aaliyah gave the word, Lady was content to amble along at the rear of the pack, enjoying the scenery. Alphonse appreciated that in a horse.

The hounds were let loose and immediately bolted off in a joyful cacophony of barks, and the hunting party whooped and cheered as they egged their horses after them. Aaliyah reined in her mount without more than a token protest from the horse.

"I thought we might go our own way," she called to Alphonse over the din. "So as to talk away from all this nonsense."

"Yes, please!"

With a grin, she touched her heels to her horse's sides, and the mare was off like lightning, leaping straight into a gallop and heading away from the hunt at an angle. With a curse, Alphonse urged Lady after her, giving chase across the hills.

It was easy to treat Aaliyah as one of the lads when she pulled such stunts as this, Alphonse thought, coaxing Lady on faster as Aaliyah thundered ahead, the grey's tail waving like a banner. The ground was firm underfoot, and the horses' hooves sent clods of earth flying up with every stride, their flanks heaving as the sun shone overhead. The sky was a perfect blue, dotted with clouds like cotton batting, and as Alphonse's heart thudded in time with the hoofbeats, he experienced a second of perfect clarity. The air, the green, the company: that was what it was all about. Not the politics of marriage, or the threats of overbearing mothers, or the old hurt of not meaning enough to somebody. He had everything he needed. In that second, he imagined a different life for himself: one where he was less of a disappointment to his mother, one where he had magic, and he was respected amongst his peers.

And among those peers was Jacobi: sleek, stylish Jacobi, with his perfectly slicked-back hair and his clever hands, dressed in spotless black, as always, but in a fine suit rather than the modest uniform of a valet. And he was riding alongside them, as flawless a horseman as he was everything else, flashing a grin at Alphonse under the bright sun. Alphonse had never seen him grin. Smile, certainly, but that was always a subtle expression, a mere curving of the mouth, eyes downcast. He'd never heard him laugh, and that suddenly struck him as being terribly unfair. He'd never heard Jacobi call him by his name, either, though that thought brought on that sense of déjà vu again, and if he really concentrated, he could almost hear the echo of his name in Jacobi's mouth, impossible as it was.

Aaliyah slowed from her gallop and turned her mare, and Alphonse shook himself free of his daydream as Lady slowed in turn.

"I say, you'd have been at the front of the pack if we'd ridden in the right direction."

She laughed, coming up alongside him. Their horses touched noses before settling in side by side, close enough for their riders' knees to jostle, heading off at a walk over the crest of a hill.

"I much prefer a solitary ride than getting caught up in the mess of a poorly organised hunt. No offense to your friends, but they've more enthusiasm than skill."

"None taken at all. I can't say I'm upset to be missing out on it myself. I don't care much for the countryside, but there's nothing like a brisk ride to clear the head, what? And I always sleep like a rock after a day of nature and fresh air."

"You don't strike me as the sort to have much trouble sleeping."

"Oh, not at all! My head touches the pillow and I'm out like a light, most often. But recently, I've been having the strangest dreams. Not bad ones, necessarily, but dashed confounding, and I've not felt as well rested as a result."

"Do you suppose it's the stress of the engagement?"

"It could be. I was awfully upset about Mother's ultimatum, I'll make no secret of it. But you've been very good about reassuring me on the subject, and I've been trying to wrap my head around the inevitability of it all. I mean, I could hardly go on as a bachelor forever, could I?"

"Some men do."

"It's not a good look, though, is it? Confirmed bachelorhood, it's called. I'd hardly mind it, but, well. People talk, and Mother's never liked things like that."

"May I ask what the dreams are about?"

"Oh, all the usual stress dreams, which are to be expected. Turning up unprepared for an exam I wrote years ago, or trying to run when my legs won't cooperate, or having my car flooded with fish. That sort of thing."

"And those are the confounding ones?"

"No." Alphonse squirmed in his saddle for a moment, debating how far he wanted to open up to her. But they were so close already, and only going to get closer, surely. In for a penny, in for a pound, as they say. "It's the strangest thing. Apart from the stress dreams, the rest are all about Jacobi."

Aaliyah's lips curled in a secret smile. "Is that so?"

"It isn't unusual in itself, what with him being there all the time. Only natural that he should seep into the old subconscious, what? I suppose they started sometime prior to this engagement business; now that I come to think, I can't say how long they've been going on. I so rarely remember my dreams, you see, but lately these ones have been following me into the day, and I feel like I've had more of them than I can recall. In any case, they've grown more vivid lately, and that's why I remember them better. I wouldn't remark on them at all, except that in the dreams, Jacobi's not quite himself. Or perhaps I'm not quite myself? It all feels perfectly natural while I'm in them. It's only after I wake up that I realise it's not right at all. Like looking through a window into another life."

A little hedge cropped up, separating one field from the next, and Aaliyah led them along its border, letting the horses amble at a leisurely pace.

"How so?" she asked.

"Well, it's going to sound terribly odd, so I must ask you to keep it between us. We do have that understanding, don't we?" he added, suddenly anxious. "What with everything else, the engagement being what it is—"

"Quite confidential," Aaliyah said firmly. "Alphonse, please. Whatever you want to tell me, I have no intention of judging you for it." She paused. "Well, I might judge you, but no more than I judge you for anything else."

"Right. Well. It's just that, in these dreams, we're rather peers? I mean to say, he's very much my equal, on even footing for once, and we're flatmates rather than a young master and his valet, and it's all very *comfortable*, really, is the only word for it. Like we're old friends. And he's got magic in this other life, and it's the most natural thing in the world, watching him do it. And then, when I wake up after this spot of domestic bliss, I feel so awfully blue that it's not real. Only for a second, mind—I'm not given to such moods, you know, not suited for them at all—but in that second, I could really believe that it's a tragedy to be waking up to this life and not that one." He ducked his head, feeling pink again, and not wanting to meet her gaze to see what was in her expression. "So, there you have it. Odd, what?"

"Like you said, Jacobi has been in your life for quite some time. It's not unusual for him to occupy your thoughts."

"No, it's just that— Well, it's hardly befitting a young master to be so preoccupied with the help." He chewed on the inside of his cheek for a second. "That's not it. That's what Mother would say. No: it feels off on account of our natures, you see. Because we're not equals, are we? And we never will be."

He chanced a glance sideways. Aaliyah seemed about to speak, her expression similar to the chilly dismissive one she had worn when talking to Featherstrop, and suddenly it was imperative that she never view Alphonse as poorly as she did him.

"He's so dashed clever!" he blurted. "And organised, and unflappable. You could drop him in the middle of anything, any time, and he'd have it sorted in minutes. It's an absolute waste to have him serving chaps such as myself all his life. He could be running the country, if only he were born to the right family. Meanwhile, here I am, wittering my life away with nothing to show for it."

Blowing out his breath and feeling somewhat better for getting that out, he glanced back at his companion. Aaliyah no longer looked cross with him, thank god.

"I should hardly say he's a good fit for politics," she said, with a quirk of her mouth. "He seems far too good a soul for it."

"That, too! He's kind, and gentle, and relentlessly focused. Don't get me wrong, I count myself jolly lucky to have him. The luckiest chap in the world, I should say. But I can't help but feel that, in some other world, he could have done something great with himself. And here I am, dragging him down. Who wants to spend their life ironing the suits of some young airhead?

Especially someone with potential like that? It absolutely baffles me, why he's stayed as long as he has. Even if he's doomed to remain a valet forever, he could find a far better employer, I'm sure. Dash it all, I'd help him do it, if he asked."

Aaliyah was staring at him. He'd rambled on too long. Before he could change the subject to something lighter, she said, "Do you really not know why he stays?"

He opened his mouth. Nothing came out, so he shut it again.

"Oh, for—" She shook her head. "Alphonse. *Alphonse.*"

"What?"

"Thank god you're pretty."

"People often tell me that."

Laughing helplessly, she rode on ahead. Alphonse made no attempt to catch her. People often found themselves needing space around him, and he understood. After a moment, she wheeled her horse around to face him, bringing them both to a halt.

"Alphonse. May I ask you a potentially uncomfortable question?"

"Er, yes, I suppose."

"You say you were in love with Featherstrop, back in the day. How did you know?"

Alphonse blinked. "Well, I suppose it was just…the feeling, wasn't it? All embarrassed and hot under the collar, thinking about him constantly, making up excuses to steal time with him alone. That sort of thing. I thought it was love. It's certainly the closest I've ever been to love, in any case. I've never felt a rush like it since, but then, I've never really gone looking, either. It's much more difficult for a chap once he's out in the real world, and of course the real world's not so forgiving to that sort of activity. So."

Aaliyah brought her horse up so they were side by side once more, the grey's nose pointed towards Lady's tail.

"Do you still have feelings for him?"

"Oh, no, not like that. There's a residual fondness, but it's all muddled over now." He sniffed. "It's hard to have feelings for a chap when he's so dismissive of it all. And of course, now that I'm older, I know he's a bit of an arse. That was easier to overlook, back in the day. A lot of things were, really."

"Did you ever dream of having a life together?" she asked curiously.

"What? Heavens, no! I dreamed about—erm." He blushed a furious red and she laughed. "I mean to say. Hardly appropriate conversation, what?"

"We're engaged," she reminded him, reaching over to squeeze his hand. "Everyone already thinks we're being inappropriate with one another, or that we're about to be."

"Yes, but that's— You can't ask a chap about that sort of dream! And anyway, that was a long time ago. I never imagined us together in any sort of, of domestic relationship. It was just a lot of kissing, and…and wandering hands, and whatnot. You know. Schoolboy fantasies."

"Not how you dream about Jacobi, then."

Alphonse took a minute to really think that over. He'd never dreamed of kissing Jacobi, and certainly never anything more than that, but he had wanted to, hadn't he? He couldn't remember the details of it, but there was a warm ball of yearning in his chest when he thought about those cottage dreams that were somehow more intimate than the explicit fantasies he'd once entertained of Featherstrop. His dreams of Jacobi were quiet, and sweet, and filled with such simple contentment that when he woke, he was filled with awful longing, even though Jacobi was right there with him, day after day.

"I say," he said softly. "Aaliyah. Do you think I'm in love with Jacobi?"

"I think there's a distinct possibility, yes."

"I say," he repeated. His head felt hollowed out and his brain replaced with wool, so baffled was he by this realisation. It made perfect sense, of course, but what on earth was he meant to do about it? He couldn't very well take the problem of his newfound love to Jacobi, his main problem-solver, for that would only introduce a whole new set of obstacles.

"Dash it all," he said faintly. "I think you're right, but I'm not nearly well enough equipped to deal with it."

"Give it a moment to settle," she suggested, letting go of his hand to turn her horse around and point her into the field again. "Is it a problem, do you think?"

"It would only be a problem if I acted on it, and I can't imagine doing anything like that. It's not right for a gentleman to go after the staff, not when they're on his payroll. Simply not right at all."

"In this other life, where the two of you are equals. Do you think that version of Jacobi would object?"

Before Alphonse could decide on an answer, the hedge shivered and a rabbit darted out under Lady's hooves, like a flash of tawny lightning. Lady spooked, jerking away from the offending rabbit, and Alphonse, wholly unprepared for such sudden movement, pitched straight over her neck and into the hedge with a yelp. His backside collided hard with the ground underneath while his limbs got stuck in the hedge's top branches, so that he was very effectively trapped in place. Lady, once assured that the rabbit had rabbited off, ambled over to give him a curious whuff, her muzzle investigating his hair, as if she were confused as to why he was on the ground when he should have been on her back. When he didn't immediately right himself, she gave the horsey equivalent of a shrug, and moseyed off to find something to nibble.

Alphonse's limbs were all entangled in the shrubbery, its spindly branches clinging to his clothes and scratching the backs of his hands. Like a beetle trapped wrong-side up, he couldn't find a way to right himself, and his helpless flailing only ensnared him further.

Simultaneously laughing and wearing an expression of concern, Aaliyah brought her mare up alongside him, bending down from her saddle to grasp his hands and haul him upright. Once out of the hedge, Alphonse doubled over, wincing, to brace his hands on his knees.

"Are you hurt at all?"

"Only battered, I think."

Gingerly, he patted himself down. Only a few scratches, but he felt sore all over. His bottom had borne the brunt of his impact, and his muscles were already beginning to ache, but there were no bones poking out of places they shouldn't have been, and therefore nothing stopping him from limping his way back to the house.

"Perhaps we'll cut our part in the hunt short, what? Head back for a spot of lunch? A stiff drink? What?" he asked hopefully.

"Stand up and walk a few yards," Aaliyah ordered. "Let me see that you're all in one piece."

Groaning, Alphonse obliged, gingerly hobbling his way in the direction she pointed. It hurt an awful lot, but he was sure his injuries were minor. If he'd any pride, it would have taken a bigger hit than his body, he was certain.

"Can you ride back to the house, do you think?"

He patted both hands over his rump and immediately winced. That was going to bruise, no doubt about it. His tailbone felt like it had been bludgeoned with a blunt object.

"I don't love that idea," he admitted. "Walking's going to take a jolly long time at this pace, though. I don't suppose you could rig me up a sled of some sort, like a litter out of branches or something, and pull me behind you?"

"No," said Aaliyah, "I'm not going to do that. But I can give you something to take the edge off until we get back, if you like."

"Oh god, please."

CHAPTER SIX

IN WHICH ALPHONSE IS VERY MUCH UNDER THE INFLUENCE OF BOTH LOVE AND QUESTIONABLE HERBAL REMEDIES

Hopping down from the saddle, Aaliyah fished through her pockets to withdraw a folded handkerchief. Confused, Alphonse held out one hand, and she opened the cloth to reveal a cluster of dried plant matter, a pinch of which she deposited in his upturned palm. The stuff was crumbly and dark red, almost brown, with the tiniest speck of yellow dotting it here and there.

"God's Tongue," she said brightly. "I always keep a spot on me, just in case. This is just the leaves, so it shouldn't hit you as hard as the flower might."

Withdrawing a flask from another pocket, she pressed that into his hand as well. "This is water. You don't want to mix alcohol with God's Tongue. You don't want to mix anything with it, actually."

"No matter. I'm sore enough that I'd take a horse tranquilizer, if I could." He tipped the contents of his palm into his open mouth, grimacing at the bitter taste. "Eugh, blech. That's not pleasant at all, is it?"

As soon as the words were out of his mouth the aftertaste set in, shockingly spicy—not like a hot pepper, but like the heat of too much cinnamon. He gulped the water down frantically, then set about panting, trying to cool his tongue.

"The heat will pass, and you'll start to feel better right away." Aaliyah watched him for a few more seconds before shaking her head. "Come on, you poor thing. I'll give you a leg up."

Open-mouthed and starting to sweat, Alphonse let her catch Lady before grasping hold of the saddle, set one boot in Aaliyah's proffered hand, and hoisted himself up, absolutely gracelessly.

"Oof," he groaned.

"Steady on." She swung back into her saddle like she'd been born riding. "It'll be a long trek back to the house if we're taking it at a walk, though that pain relief should hit any minute."

"I should hope so. I feel like I've been tenderised."

They made their way back to the house at a snail's pace, and every step of it was agony to Alphonse's abused body. Sitting in the saddle was uncomfortable, but standing in the stirrups was somehow worse, and though Lady was a gentle creature with a level gait, it wasn't level enough to keep from jostling him. Apart from her initial reaction of helping him out of the hedge and plying him with drugs, Aaliyah didn't seem awfully sympathetic, and was as likely to laugh at his moans as she was to wince. When the house finally came into sight, Alphonse nearly fell from the saddle again in sheer boneless relief.

"I'll ride ahead and find Jacobi," she offered, trotting away before he could beg her to stay.

It wasn't that he needed company so much as someone to help him down. The ground had never looked so far away. He could always wait until Jacobi arrived to rescue him, but he found he would rather embarrass himself in front of his fiancée than in front of his valet, which was entirely backwards, except for the fact that he was in love with the latter rather than the former.

"Lord above," he breathed, slumping forward to drape himself over Lady's neck. She flicked her ears back to listen, but otherwise stood agreeably still. "How did that happen, old girl? *When* did that happen?"

He was vaguely aware that whatever Aaliyah had given him was beginning to take effect, and that it was considerably stronger than any pharmaceutical pain killer he had ever come across. His body first went very heavy—hence the draping—and then incredibly light, so light he could have been floating, and with his body went his brain. His mind wandered off, as airy as a cloud drifting through the perfect blue of the sky, and though he grabbed for it, it slipped between his fingers with a cheerful wave.

Well, he was used to getting by without much brain. Perhaps he wouldn't miss the last of it.

"This is fine," he said aloud, and slithered sideways out of the saddle, grasping ineffectively at Lady's mane as he dropped, seemingly in slow motion, to the ground. For all his lightness, his knees gave out immediately, and he landed in a crumpled heap underneath her. His body, it must be noted, did not feel the impact.

"Jolly powerful herbs," he informed Lady's hooves. "Really spiffing stuff."

Getting his legs back under him, he dragged himself upright with the help of the right stirrup, flinging one arm around her neck to use her as a crutch as he pointed them both at the house.

"Onward," he told her, with determination. Sighing, she indulged him, walking along at a steady pace and allowing him to lean his full weight against her side.

Aaliyah found them outside the stable, with Jacobi at her heels like a shadow.

"Ah!" Alphonse cried, delighted to see them both until he recalled that those amorous feelings needed to be organized and dealt with first, lest they come tumbling out of his mouth unchecked. "Ah," he repeated, with more alarm, for he was in no state to be processing said feelings whatsoever. "Aaliyah, what did you say those flowers were called? The ones you gave me?"

"I'm afraid I don't know what you call them in Britain," she said, with a cagey glance at Jacobi.

"Tonguey something, aren't they? Rather strong, what?"

"That's not God's Tongue, is it, Miss Kaddour?" Jacobi asked.

Alphonse flapped a hand at him. "That's the one! God's Tongue. She showed them to me that time at Kew; I remember now. Brilliant red plant, very flashy. Spicy as all get out, I can tell you."

"Medicinal God's Tongue has never been approved for distribution in Britain, sir," Jacobi said, concern flashing in his eyes.

"Ah," said Aaliyah. "Has it not."

A groom appeared to detach Alphonse from Lady's side, leading her away, and he wavered for a moment before deciding it would be easier to simply sit down where he was, in a patch of hay-strewn dirt.

"Sir? You didn't hit your head when you fell?"

"Not a bit," Alphonse assured Jacobi. "But my legs are rather less cooperative than normal, so I thought I'd just have a sit-down, and try again in a bit."

"I'm so sorry," Aaliyah said, not really looking it. "I only meant to take the edge off his aches, but it must have hit him harder than I anticipated."

"Sir, if I may suggest we move your sit-down to the indoors? A chaise, perhaps?"

"Oh, don't trouble yourself, old thing. I'm quite comfortable down here."

Jacobi looked pained. Alphonse had never been good at resisting anything Jacobi suggested, so he sighed and held out one arm. "Alright, inside it is."

"Thank you, sir."

It was only when Jacobi had clasped hold of his hand that Alphonse realized the man didn't mean to merely pull him to his feet, but to carry him inside like a proper invalid.

"I say!" Alphonse yelped, as Jacobi settled him over his shoulder.

"Forgive me, sir, but if your legs aren't cooperating—"

"I could use you as a crutch!"

"I'm considerably smaller than the horse, sir. Unless you would prefer I carry you in some other manner?"

The only other alternative Alphonse could picture was as a groom might carry his new bride, and though the thought filled him with a pleasant rush of heat, he had just enough mental capacity remaining to know it was a bad idea.

"Like a sack of flour it is," he said, with as much dignity as he could muster.

Aaliyah followed a step behind Jacobi, perhaps to keep Alphonse's head company as Jacobi steered him foot-first into the house.

"How are you feeling, Alphonse?" she asked as they crossed the threshold. "I really didn't imagine you would have such a strong reaction, or I'd never have given it to you. As small a dose as it was."

"I feel wonderful, present position notwithstanding, but I'm not convinced that's a good thing."

"No?"

"No. You see, what we talked about, just prior to my ending up in the hedge—"

"Yes, of course—"

"It's a delicate matter," he told her as Jacobi carried him down the corridor to the sitting room. Or, rather, he told her midsection, for her face was somewhere above his field of vision. "And I don't feel up to delicacy, at the moment. I feel rather like a hot air balloon, what? Except the hot air is all the secrets that I'm meant to keep inside the balloony bit, and instead, I'm as likely to spill them all over the place as I am to go floating off into space. It's a terrible mess."

Finding one of his hands, she clasped it encouragingly as they turned the corner into the room. "I'm terribly sorry, but I think your secrets are quite safe in present company."

"What? No! No, they're absolutely not safe in present company! How on earth could you say such a thing?"

Upset, he began wriggling like an indignant fish, and only stopped when Jacobi deposited him in a tangle of limbs on a chaise. The sitting room was a bright, airy place with a wall of windows overlooking the greenery. The hunt was too far off to hear, but Alphonse could imagine the bell-like barking of the hounds all the same, and hoped they might return sooner than later and provide a helpful distraction before he accidentally vomited his heart all over his unsuspecting valet.

"Sir." Jacobi smoothed the lines of his suit, stepping back and averting his gaze. "If you would like me to go until you can regain some sobriety of mind—"

"Wait! No, no, I don't want you to leave. I only—" Alphonse cast a beseeching look at Aaliyah, who shrugged unhelpfully.

"I could fetch you something to eat, sir," Jacobi offered, clearly looking for any excuse to leave his mess of a young master to recover himself.

"Water," Aaliyah suggested. "To flush the drug from his system."

"Yes, ma'am."

Jacobi shimmered off, leaving Alphonse under Aaliyah's supervision.

"This is how I ended up here in the first place," he told her, without much accusation. "Left to your tender mercies."

"Would you like me to go?"

He struggled upright with a wind-milling of arms. "And leave me with him? No! All of you, stop abandoning me to one another."

Kneeling by the chaise, Aaliyah pressed him back as if she could make him relax through sheer force of will. "No one is abandoning you, and there's no reason to come over all shy. Nothing has changed between you and Jacobi."

"Everything has changed!" he said in a strangled whisper. "How am I supposed to keep from blurting it out in front of him? All I can think about is how it would be to kiss him! You've conflated all these different dreams in my head, and now I'm terribly confused!"

He had never thought about kissing Jacobi before, but now, he could imagine nothing else. Jacobi's lips were thin, but perfectly sculpted, given to wry acknowledgements and gentle admonishments, and were always the perfect shade of dark pink, and never chapped. Alphonse wanted to kiss him there, and on his knuckles, and perhaps even in secret places hidden by his suit. Alphonse had never seen him without his suit, not in all the years they had lived together, and suddenly, seeing him stripped down to his underthings—his mind was flighty and couldn't land on the thought of stripping him completely bare, not yet—was of the utmost importance. Jacobi had seen Alphonse in his underthings often enough, after all. How would it feel to have Jacobi's hands linger rather than move with brisk efficiency? How would it feel to press their lips together, and have Jacobi return the kiss as ardently as Alphonse offered it?

"You've gone pink again," Aaliyah noted.

Alphonse smothered himself with a decorative cushion.

"Look," Aaliyah said, calmly leaving him to it, "just focus on your injuries. If he asks you a question, tell him about how much everything hurts. It will keep you both distracted."

"That won't work," Alphonse said, through the smothering.

"Then pretend that you hit your head after all, and go unconscious for a while. He'll panic and call the doctor, of course, but if you really can't risk speaking to him—"

Alphonse dropped the cushion. "Don't be absurd. Jacobi has never panicked about anything in his life."

Jacobi chose that moment to reappear in the doorway, offering Alphonse a glass of water. "Sir. Did you decide whether you wanted anything to eat?"

"I did, and I don't."

"Sir?"

Jacobi was perfect. His suit, his hair, those lovely dark eyes that were always brimming with unspoken humour or careful disdain. His eyelashes, the kind girls and movie stars would go mad to have, and the graceful arch of his brows, so reserved in their expression, but so easy to read after five years of studying their movement. God above, how had Alphonse never realised it before? Of course he was in love with the man! Dreams of domestic bliss— He had been absolutely oblivious to his own subconscious workings for weeks, if not months! Hell, he had probably been half in love with the man from the moment he set foot in the door!

"I'm dying, you see," Alphonse blurted, "so it seems a waste of good food."

Aaliyah delicately covered her mouth with one hand.

Jacobi lifted one eyebrow, and the sardonic judgement was as evident as if he had voiced it aloud. "Dying, sir."

"Yes. I've broken every bone in my body, and I shall have to be entombed in this very chaise. I'm never to move again."

"I don't think that's true, sir."

"Tell him, Aaliyah! Aren't I dying?"

"He does seem considerably moribund. Might I suggest wrapping him up in a comfortable shroud and taking him home, where he might pass in peace?"

"Ma'am," Jacobi said, with the mildest reproach.

"Or, if you were to gently nurse him back to health, you might find that he makes a miraculous recovery."

Alphonse squawked and thumped her with the cushion.

Jacobi considered them both. "Am I to understand that the fall was worse than it appeared?"

"The fall, or the drugs."

Alphonse rallied. "No need to bother with the nursing or the shroud, thank you, Jacobi, for I feel like I've already died. I'm in shambles. A mere corpse." To prove his point, he flopped sideways over the chaise, head lolling and arms limp, one trailing to the floor.

"I see. Are you sure a small sandwich wouldn't make you feel better, sir?"

Alphonse paused in his death throes. "It might. What kind have you got?"

"There are roast chicken, cheese and cucumber, and egg on offer, sir. Shall I bring you one after all?"

He couldn't help it. Under the confusingly romantic feelings and the haze of drugs, he was hungry after the ride. "Cucumber, if you please. That sounds awfully refreshing. Just what I need in my current state."

"Your state of shambles, sir?"

"Yes, precisely."

THE BACHELOR'S VALET

As Jacobi disappeared again to find the sandwich in question, Aaliyah helped Alphonse back to a seated position, ignoring the little sound he made as his sore backside made contact with the cushions.

"Gently nursing me back to health," he muttered. "That's just the sort of thing I don't need to be thinking about, you devil!"

"Oh, hush. I'm doing you a favour."

"You most certainly are not!"

Jacobi returned with the sandwich considerably faster than he had returned with the water, perhaps assuming that Alphonse was no longer avoiding his company. For his part, Alphonse hardly knew what he wanted. He relied so much on Jacobi to tell him what was good for him that to remove Jacobi from the equation was to leave him treading water in circles, and he suspected that trying to replace Jacobi with Aaliyah would lead to ruin. And, furthermore, that she would enjoy herself as she led him astray.

"You're a terrible influence," he told her, taking the sandwich with clumsy hands. His fingers felt very thick, and very floppy. "I can't believe we're to be married."

"You'll be grateful for it, eventually."

"Ugh, I say."

He crunched into the sandwich to avoid having to speak any more, and realised that he should have demanded food from the start. The cucumber was delightfully cool and crisp, the cream cheese slathered on thick, and he moved it around in his mouth long after he was done chewing, marvelling at the texture of it all.

"Sir," Jacobi said eventually. "Glad as I am to see you enjoying your lunch, if we might move things along...?"

Alphonse swallowed thickly and wiped his mouth with the back of one hand, guiltily ignoring Jacobi's wince. "Right, right. Sorry, old chap. Terrible manners. You should have left me in the barn after all."

"Sir, if I may. I think Miss Kaddour is right, and you would recuperate better at home."

Home alone with Jacobi seemed a dangerous idea, though the longer he dwelled on it, the further off the danger got, wandering away from him as easily as his concentration. In fact, the longer he lounged on the chaise, limbs akimbo and body melting into the cushions, the less serious anything seemed. Why shouldn't he let Jacobi take him home and care for him? It was what they'd always done, after all.

No, some tiny, sober and alarmed part of his brain insisted. *No, you mustn't! There will be repercussions!*

But when he interrogated that part of his brain about what repercussions might result from entrusting himself to Jacobi, body and soul, as per usual, it couldn't offer up any good explanation, just a vague sort of embarrassed worry, which wasn't nearly enough to deter him.

Aaliyah touched his knee reassuringly. "You'll be fine. Jacobi will take good care of you."

"Of course he will. He always does." Alphonse beamed up at Jacobi, leaning over to give him a clumsy pat on the arm. Jacobi took a neat step out of reach to avoid being smeared with cream cheese. "You take the best care of me, old chap. I couldn't ask for better."

"I'm glad to hear it, sir."

"Jacobi," Aaliyah said in a low voice, drawing the man to the side for an ostensibly private moment, though well within Alphonse's earshot.

Alphonse's panic had subsided once he was fed, replaced with a warm wash of bubbly contentment which was surely bad for his impulse-control, but so much preferable to the anxious, overthinking stage of the drug that he couldn't help but lean into it, humming to himself as Aaliyah spoke to Jacobi in an undertone.

"I don't know your familiarity with God's Tongue, but it can plant strange ideas in one's head, if the user isn't accustomed to it. So, if Alphonse is acting a bit odder than usual, it's really nothing to worry about. Once he sleeps it off, he'll be back to his normal self like nothing ever happened."

"I say, it's nicer than being drunk, though, what?" Alphonse said cheerfully, blinking upside-down at them from where his head had dropped off the side of the chaise. "Oh, it's not going to leave me with an awful hangover though, is it? I've lost whole days to hangovers before, and though Jacobi makes a spiffing remedy, this isn't exactly alcohol. Different rules, I bet. Terribly unfair."

"Lots of rest and plenty of water should head it off at the pass," Aaliyah assured him, or perhaps informed Jacobi. Informing Jacobi would be more useful, so she had probably addressed him directly, seeing as she was a practical sort.

Alphonse kicked his legs up over the back of the chaise and let all the blood rush to his head. It was a fizzy sensation, not unpleasant, though Jacobi seemed pained by it.

"Sir."

"Hm?"

"I'll carry you to the car."

There was a reason for Alphonse to object to that. He ran the suggestion by his dignity and came up with an indifferent shrug, so it wasn't a matter of pride. Aaliyah looked wildly amused, which should have been a clue, but she wasn't talking, so Alphonse gave Jacobi a sunny smile and dropped his legs down to the chaise cushions again and held up one arm.

"Righto. Onwards and upwards?"

"Quite, sir."

Jacobi moved to lift Alphonse as he had done before, with one hand behind his knees in order to heft him over his shoulder, but Alphonse intercepted him by flinging both arms around Jacobi's neck. Jacobi paused for a second before recalibrating—he was ever so adaptable—and lifting Alphonse into a much more comfortable bridal carry, straightening effortlessly like Alphonse didn't weigh a thing.

"You're awfully strong, what?" Alphonse said admiringly, patting Jacobi's chest. To the side, Aaliyah covered her mouth like she was trying to hold back a laugh. "I should have you carry me everywhere. So much more convenient than me walking myself around!"

"I'm not sure that's true, sir."

"Is it not? That's a shame. It's rather comfy up here, you know. I guess you must know; you're up here all the time. It's all you, after all."

"Miss Kaddour. How long do you expect these effects to last?"

"I really only gave him a pinch of the stuff. I had no idea it would incapacitate him like this."

"Am I incapacitated?" Alphonse wondered. "I feel in tip-top shape, actually. Really spiffing! I've stopped hurting, which is brilliant, of course, and now that I don't have to worry about keeping my legs under me, I feel capable of just about anything!"

"You're not," Aaliyah told him. To Jacobi, she added, "I'd just put him to bed, if I were you. By the time he wakes up, he'll be completely recovered."

"Bedtime!" Alphonse objected. "It's the middle of the day! The sun's still out. I can see it, so don't tell you tell me it's not. It's sunny as anything."

"You're accustomed to sleeping in till noon, sir; it shouldn't be any stretch to sleep from noon to dusk."

Alphonse pondered that. It seemed eminently rational, as did all things coming from Jacobi's esteemed mouth. "I suppose you have a point."

"Thank you, sir."

"But I don't feel sleepy."

"I have hope that the drive home will change that, sir."

"Very well, then. Home, and to bed!" He brightened, and angled around to face Jacobi, who grappled him around the middle to keep him from falling. "You know, Jacobi, I've been having the most remarkable dreams about you, lately. The absolute highlight of my nights, I tell you."

"Alphonse," Aaliyah said loudly. "I think you're confusing Jacobi with someone else."

"Oh, I could never!"

"No, I really think you are." Stepping closer, she took him by the chin, and the touch startled him into immediate silence as he stared at her wide-eyed. "You hit your head a bit in that fall," she told him, enunciating as she clearly tried to beam her meaning straight into his poor beleaguered brain. "Do you remember falling into that hedge?"

"I do. It bally well hurt."

"Yes. And do you remember what we were talking about just prior?"

He stared at her. She stared back. She seemed awfully intent on broadcasting *something*, but Alphonse couldn't quite grasp—

"Oh!" he cried. And then: "*Oh*. Oh, right. Yes."

Really not something he ought to say to Jacobi; really not something he ought to say at all. How much had he said already? With his arms around the man, clinging like a limpet! Alarmed by his total lack of propriety, Alphonse reared back, trying to untangle himself from his valet. This succeeded only in unbalancing them both, Jacobi's grip slipping and prompting him to take hold of Alphonse quite firmly by the waist, hoisting him back up in a terribly undignified manner, like a cat being hauled up in the overenthusiastic embrace of a tot. Though less prone to clawing in such a circumstance, Alphonse still let out a

THE BACHELOR'S VALET

yowl at being manhandled in such a way, and gave fresh life to his struggles, squirming around in an attempt to escape.

"Sir," said Jacobi, in a tone of total exasperation. His hands were clasped around the small of Alphonse's back, his chest crushed against Alphonse's solar plexus, with Alphonse's chin grazing the top of Jacobi's head, his feet not quite touching the floor. "If I put you down, you will fall."

"Not a bit," Alphonse assured him, feeling red-faced and hot all over. "Rather intimate, what?" he couldn't help but add, and then, mortified, went limp and noodled straight down out of Jacobi's arms to puddle onto the floor.

"This is ridiculous," Aaliyah announced. "Thank you for the outing, Alphonse, but I'm going to leave now. I'll get a ride back into the city from someone else, and call round tomorrow to see that you've survived."

"Aaliyah?" Alphonse called mournfully from Jacobi's ankles. "Aaliyah, I think I'm in trouble."

"You are a bit, and I'm sorry for it, but I'm sure it'll all work out. Bye for now."

"Toodles," he said sadly, watching her boots go marching from the room. Rolling onto his back, he folded his hands over his chest and stared up at the ceiling, which was soon obscured by Jacobi's visage as he leaned over his master's prone form. "I suppose you'd better take me home. I've gone all wobbly, I'm afraid."

"Would you like to check in with a doctor, sir?"

"No, no. I'm sure Aaliyah's got the right of it."

"She should never have given you that drug, sir. There's good reason it's not distributed in Britain."

"I do feel awfully nice, is the thing," Alphonse admitted, drumming his fingers over his ribs. "Not a care in the world. Except for... except for that thing I'm not meant to tell you." He blinked up at Jacobi, the thinnest thread of anxiety winding through him. "Aaliyah was helping me keep it hush hush, but now that she's gone, I do worry that I'm going to spill it all over you, and I really shouldn't. It's not right."

"Then I advise you to stop speaking, sir," Jacobi said tiredly.

"I've always been rubbish at that. Not talking. Never took to it."

"I know, sir."

"Could you maybe stop listening, instead?" Alphonse asked, with a flare of hope. "Aaliyah told you the drug muddled my brain right up, didn't she? I feel like I'm talking nonsense. You mustn't listen to anything I say right now. Just disregard all of it until I've sobered up."

"If you think that best, sir. Would you like to try standing, or shall I pick you up again?"

Alphonse considered that, idly curling one hand around Jacobi's ankle, his thumb finding the protruding bone. He could use Jacobi to lever himself upright, but that would involve far more physical contact than seemed right. There was no winning.

"I'm comfortable here, actually, and might just lay on the floor until I've regained my senses."

"I must advise against it, sir," said Jacobi, and, kneeling, scooped Alphonse up like a babe.

Evidently having learned from his previous mistake, he wasted no time in whisking Alphonse from the sitting room, striding briskly down the wide hall with its many framed artistic endeavours, to the foyer, where a cluster of youths mingled around, having returned early from the hunt. Alphonse smiled brightly at all of them, his head lolling against Jacobi's arm. He had mentioned before how strong Jacobi was to lift him so effortlessly, but really, he needed to comment on it again, the easy muscle the man hid under his suit. So distracted, Alphonse almost missed Featherstrop as he walked by.

"I say!" Alphonse called loudly, hit by a bolt of inspiration. Both Jacobi and Featherstrop paused, Featherstrop looking attentive, if confused, and Jacobi long-suffering. "I say," Alphonse repeated, "Featherstrop, old thing. I wanted to catch you before I left."

"Are you quite alright there, chap? You seem a bit…"

"I had a fall! A fall, and an—an inebriation, following it, what?"

"Ah, sorry to hear it. You're heading off early, then?"

"I am," Alphonse confirmed, "but I wanted to give you a piece of my mind, before I did."

"Oh?"

"Sir," Jacobi interjected in a low voice, "this perhaps isn't a piece of mind you wish to share in earshot of so many people. Or, perhaps, at all."

"Not so! Featherstrop, old thing, chap: I only wanted to tell you that I deserved better than you, actually, and if I weren't such a sap, I'd have seen it years earlier! I just hope you treat your girl better than you treated *mff—*"

Jacobi neatly placed one hand over Alphonse's mouth. "I do apologise, Mr. Featherstrop. Mr. Hollyhock is unwell, and his words aren't to be taken seriously at this time."

"Mff!" Alphonse objected, wetly, against Jacobi's palm.

"Right," Featherstrop said faintly. "Jolly good. I'll hope for a speedy recovery then, what?"

"Thank you, sir. I'm sure Mr. Hollyhock would appreciate that, if he were of a clearer mind."

Alphonse tried to bite the offending hand, but Jacobi merely smiled politely at their host before hauling Alphonse bodily out the door and away from their gathering audience.

CHAPTER SEVEN

AN UNCOMFORTABLE CONVERSATION IN WHICH TOO MUCH IS LEFT UNSAID

Jacobi didn't relent until Alphonse was packed into the passenger seat of the car with the door shut firmly behind him. Only then did he withdraw and allow Alphonse to wipe his mouth with the back of one sleeve, scowling mightily, as much from the indignity of his exit as from the sudden lack of Jacobi's body against his.

"You should have let me finish. I had a lot more to tell him."

"I was instructed to disregard everything you had to say, sir," Jacobi said as he slid into the driver's seat and turned the engine to life. "I inferred, therefore, that your intentions were to be likewise mistrusted, and best thwarted."

"That's not right at all!" Alphonse twisted around in his seat, glaring back at the house through the rear window. "I was so looking forward to telling him what for. I'd finally figured out the measure of him, and then you—thwarted!" He sat straight and crossed his arms with a harrumph.

"If you're of a similar mind tomorrow, you're welcome to finish the conversation, sir." Jacobi kept his eyes fixed on the view through the windshield as he pulled out of the long estate drive and onto the road proper, heading back towards the city. "But until then, I strongly suggest you keep your thoughts and opinions to yourself."

"Ugh," said Alphonse, settling deeper into his seat for a good sulk, but once he was settled, he found his eyelids growing heavy and his body coming over all floaty again. "I expect you're right," he allowed grudgingly. "You usually are, about most things." Rolling his head to the side, he blinked at Jacobi, the bright afternoon sun catching in his lashes and, to his addled brain, making Jacobi seem painted in starry gold, all a-glimmer. "That's why I like you so much," he explained, his voice slipping into a tone far too sincere, and he was helpless to stop it. "Your dependability, you see. Absolutely steadfast in all ways. It's not many chaps who can say they've got such a stalwart companion by their side, and I don't take it for granted. Not a bit."

THE BACHELOR'S VALET

Cracking a yawn, he covered his mouth with one hand before getting distracted by the way the light slanted down in between his fingers. And from there, how it landed on Jacobi, its touch as light as a lover's, painting him in delicate sheets of sunbeams like an old master's portrait of royalty from centuries past. Alphonse stared at him, his mouth slightly open, though no words came out, with his heart shining from his eyes. Jacobi cast him a brief glance before returning his attention to the road. Alphonse couldn't tell what Jacobi saw in him in that moment, but he knew he ought to mask it. It did no good, wearing one's emotions so plainly on the face like that, especially not so inappropriate an emotion as love. Not that love was inappropriate in itself: to the contrary! But for a gentleman to feel that way about his valet— Except that, with his mind so baffled by the God's Tongue, it didn't feel like something that needed to be hidden away at all.

"Jacobi," he began.

"Sir," Jacobi said softly. "Please don't."

Alphonse shut his mouth, unaccountably hurt, and tucked himself into as small a space as he could manage on his side of the car, his temple pressed to the window as the scenery whooshed by. He lost time gazing at the hills and trees, leaves turning to burnished auburn in the sun, each individual speck of matter catching the light and making the countryside glow warm like stained glass. If he wasn't to look at Jacobi then he'd look to nature, but the view wasn't nearly as pleasing. Funny, to have the whole world at his feet, all of nature and London to look at or find company in, and all he wanted was Jacobi. Funny that he'd never realised it sooner. Funnier still, the way that realisation kept slipping around inside his brain like a bar of soap he struggled to keep hold of in the bath. It wouldn't be funny at all if, when he next woke sober and level-headed once more, he found the realisation had escaped his grasp to go swimming down the drain, leaving him as clueless to the workings of his heart as ever before.

"I don't mean to upset you," he said quietly, as they soared into London.

"I know you don't, sir."

"It's just that I can't recall the last time I had to work through a problem without you, much less a problem that set us at odds."

"Are we at odds, sir?" Jacobi asked as he pulled into the parking garage.

Alphonse shut his eyes as the blue shadows of the underground rolled over him. "I think we must be. Otherwise you wouldn't be using that tone with me, and I wouldn't be…" He lifted one hand, turned the wrist in a vague motion. "I wouldn't be so confused, would I? I'd just be bobbing along in your wake, as always, not a care in the world."

"You only feel this way because of the drugs, sir." Jacobi parked the car and turned off the engine, pausing then to face Alphonse. "It's a temporary confusion, I assure you."

"The thing is." Alphonse swallowed thickly, sitting up and leaning forward like he could convince Jacobi of his earnestness through his posture, though he found that once he was in the position, he couldn't meet the man's eyes. "The thing is, I don't know if I want it to be temporary. I keep thinking about how your sentences would sound if you stopped peppering those *sirs* all through them, and how my name would sound in your mouth." He drew a shaky breath. "My given name, I mean. And, and what it might be like if you were to—"

Wetting his lips, his gaze stuttered up to meet Jacobi's for the first time since they had re-entered the city. He was wide-eyed and staring, he could feel it, pupils blown into hapless drowning pools. He looked the fool, surely, but then, surely he always did? But Jacobi didn't always return his look in such a specific way, with emotion writ so clearly on his face, like he was looking at something awful and pitiable. Like Alphonse had carved his still-beating heart out of his chest, offering it to his valet with both hands like a child offering his nanny an unwanted garden toad.

Jacobi's lips parted seemingly of their own accord, and for an earth-stopping second, Alphonse thought that Jacobi might say his name, those two syllables held tenderly on his tongue—

But, "You're not well, sir," were the words that came from Jacobi's mouth, and Alphonse's heart, still held securely in his chest, sank like a stone to the bottom of that unfortunate toad's pond. "And, while it's all very good to tell me to disregard your words, it's difficult, sir. More difficult than you realise, when you say such things."

Alphonse opened his mouth to apologise again, but Jacobi shook his head sharply and exited his side of the car, effectively ending the conversation. "You mustn't talk this way, sir," he said firmly, rounding the car to open Alphonse's door. "Not when there's a chance you'll regret it tomorrow."

"I won't," Alphonse said numbly, sliding his feet from the car floor to the ground. Everything felt numb. The warm autumn sun couldn't reach him in the underground lot, its gold-making rays blocked from him, leaving everything cool and blue and deadening.

Jacobi offered Alphonse his arm, waiting patiently as he found his feet and staggered upright. Alphonse did and didn't want to be carried again, twin urges warring inside him until his body made up its own mind and slumped into Jacobi's arms.

"Let's get you inside, sir."

Alphonse leaned into him the whole ride up the lift, his cheek pressed to Jacobi's shoulder, one arm slung low around the man's waist. Jacobi stood straight and tall, his chin high as if to avoid looking at his shambles of an employer. Sighing, Alphonse nestled into the sleek fabric of Jacobi's suit, soaking up his body heat through so many layers of material. By the time they reached the top floor, Alphonse's knees had all but given out, and he had to ooze himself out of the lift and through the gate, giving the doorman a ghost of his usual smile.

"I say, are you alright, Mr. Hollyhock?"

"A spot of food poisoning, I'm afraid," Jacobi said, easing Alphonse back into an upright position and taking his weight on one side.

"Ah, sorry to hear it, sir."

THE BACHELOR'S VALET

"Thanks ever so," Alphonse warbled, feeling sorrier for himself than the doorman knew.

Jacobi shepherded him into the flat, one hand at the small of Alphonse's back. "I'll make you a tea and get you to bed, sir."

"I don't think I'll sleep."

"I can fix the tea for you as I've done before." Inside, Jacobi deposited him in an armchair before sweeping into the kitchen.

"Aaliyah said the God's Tongue oughtn't be mixed up with anything else." Alphonse dropped his head to rest against the back of the chair. "Safety concerns, and all that."

"The herbal remedies I have in stock won't interfere with the drug, I assure you, sir. And I do think you would feel much better if you slept."

"Alright, then. I trust you to know your way around these things. I just wish I did."

"You'll be fine, sir. This was a misstep you could not have anticipated."

Alphonse snorted. "The drug, no! Certainly not. The rest of it, though…" He got up from his chair to weave his way to the kitchen doorway, to which he clung in his efforts to remain standing. "Jacobi."

The man didn't look up from the kettle. "Yes, sir."

"Jacobi. The rest of it. In the car… Did I upset you, looking at you like that? However that was? Because I felt…"

"Sir." Jacobi's tone was gentle but firm, his features obscured by the steam of the whistling kettle. "You should sleep this off. I'm sure you'll feel more yourself in a few hours."

"But I feel very much myself right now, Jacobi. Overwhelmingly so. I feel more myself than I ever have." Alphonse paused, an unhappy sensation curling in his stomach. "Do I not seem myself?"

Jacobi sighed, which was a great admission, coming from him. Without answering, he prepared Alphonse's tea: chamomile mint, and if he added any remedial herbs to it, Alphonse didn't see them. Setting the cup on a saucer, Jacobi waited until Alphonse pushed off from the door frame to let him pass.

"One cannot judge a man's actions when he is under the influence the same as one might when he is clear-headed, sir."

Jacobi entered Alphonse's bedroom, placing the tea on the bedside table while Alphonse stalled in the doorway for a second before deflating.

"Yes, yes. I'll go to bed. I do enjoy bedtime, you know? All tucked up, cosy as a bug. I like how you look at me, then. All warm, like. Fond. You are fond of me, aren't you, Jacobi?"

"Yes, sir. Shall I help you into your pyjamas?"

Alphonse went hot all over at the thought of Jacobi's hands on him, however professionally.

"No. I'll sleep in my clothes. Possibly on the floor. The carpet looks mighty inviting."

It did, as a matter of fact, but Jacobi cast him a judgemental look, the first direct look he'd offered since the garage, and Alphonse melted.

"Oh, alright."

THE BACHELOR'S VALET

He bit his lip as Jacobi removed his tie, teeth digging in sharp but not sharp enough to distract him from the sight of Jacobi's clever fingers at his throat. Alphonse shut his eyes, hands balled in desperate fists at his sides, but he could still *feel* everything: the heat of the man's body so near his own, the quick unbuttoning of buttons, the clean whisking off of his jacket and then the light pressure of Jacobi's palms flat against his shoulders, resting there for just a second, before moving on to his shirt. This was how he was going to die, Alphonse thought as his heart rabbited madly in his chest, so loud that surely Jacobi must hear it. But if he did, he didn't mention it, just as he didn't mention the shallowness of Alphonse's breath, or the way his body was locked up tight with tension so at odds with his earlier noodling. Alphonse had always been rubbish at keeping secrets, especially from Jacobi, but he'd never experienced this before. Telling a secret, or half-telling him, and having the man shut him down before it could even get acknowledged.

Just when Alphonse thought he could endure no more, Jacobi stepped back a pace, tutting at the pulls and scratches Alphonse's suit had accumulated during its adventure with the hedge. "I hope you walked away from your fall in better shape than your clothes, sir."

Alphonse let out a shuddering breath, loosened his hands, and opened his eyes.

"I'm sure I did," he said shakily, aiming for levity. "My backside took the worst of it, but I don't feel so bad right now. Not physically, anyway. The rest of me's rather queer, but that could be because of the whole going-to-bed-at-such-a-light-hour thing, what? Awfully queer, that."

"Yes, sir. I imagine the pains will catch up to you tomorrow, but I'm glad you sustained no worse injuries than that."

"Just bruising," Alphonse assured him.

Jacobi offered him his pyjama set, arranging the sleeves of the top so Alphonse could get his arms through them before coming back around to his front to do the buttons up, top down. It was just as excruciating being buttoned into a shirt as it was being unbuttoned out of one, but it was over faster, thank god.

"It's a rummy thing," Alphonse murmured, pulling the pyjama bottoms over his hips. He then stood transfixed for a solid minute, distracted by the soft rasp of cotton against his skin as his eyes fell shut again. "I could fall asleep standing up right here, like a horse. I could have sworn I wasn't as tired as this, but…"

"You might fall asleep that way, but I doubt you'd stay standing long. Into bed, sir."

Alphonse's eyes fluttered open to find the bedcovers turned down, the sheets crisp and inviting. "Jolly good." And then he tipped over, his upper body intent on moving forward without communicating such to his lower half, into Jacobi's waiting arms for the umpteenth time that day.

"Terribly sorry," he said into Jacobi's chest as the man steered him into bed. "Though I dare say you've seen me worse, what? Those late-night parties I used to go to? The ones with Featherstrop… We had such a cracking time at them. No, I guess that was a bit before you came on, wasn't it? But still. Better this stuff than the drink, what?"

"As you say, sir," Jacobi replied, moving Alphonse's legs from the floor to under the sheets.

Alphonse fell back against the pillows, crossing his arms as Jacobi drew the covers up to his chin, tucking him in neatly.

"Good night, sir."

"Jacobi..."

"Good night," Jacobi repeated firmly, and shut the door behind him as he departed.

Alphonse stared at the closed door. Late afternoon sun edged in around the drawn curtains, painting the room burnt orange like it used to do when Alphonse was very young, and his bedtime was before sunset in the long summer months. It had always been dashedly hard to fall asleep with the sun still in the sky, even as a tot, and he was so tempted to call Jacobi back in for conversation. Or, better yet, to call Aaliyah on the telephone and have her chat to him until he fell asleep, because *she* wasn't upset with him or his inconvenient feelings—

But between that thought and the next he fell asleep so quickly he didn't even notice it happening.

CHAPTER EIGHT

IN WHICH ALPHONSE IS TALKED OFF A LEDGE

Alphonse woke once, groggily, at eleven p.m. for just long enough to note the time, and then more permanently at four in the a.m. Unsure what he was supposed to do with himself at that hour, he dozed in bed a while longer, dropping in and out of sleep without any real commitment. He could tell that once he got up, he would be sore, but as long as he lounged around in bed, his body couldn't protest too much. Finally, propping himself up against his pillows, he took stock of his situation, first checking that all his limbs and appendages were accounted for, and then that they still worked. He was a little hazy around the edges, but miles more alert than he had been the previous afternoon, and with that alertness came the niggling suspicion that he had made an absolute fool of himself. That in itself wasn't awfully unusual; he made a fool of himself on a regular basis, in one way or another. He and foolishness were old friends. But in this case, he couldn't remember what precisely he had done, which made it harder to tell whether it was something he could laugh off, or whether he should really ask forgiveness and promise not to do it again.

He remembered falling off the horse, and limping his way back to the house with Aaliyah. He remembered…flashes, after that. Flashes of conversation, of absurd physicality, and being put to bed like a toddler in need of a nap. But the flashes did not form a cohesive narrative. He did, however, remember being informed of his attraction to Jacobi. His heart leapt for a second, as it was wont to do when faced with love, before plummeting again as the previous afternoon came barrelling back in full force.

"Jacobi," he breathed. "Oh, god, what did I say to him?"

Far too much and simultaneously not enough. He'd made his feelings clumsily known without actually managing to articulate them, such that they must have seemed like inebriated ramblings rather than a heartfelt confession. If he wanted Jacobi to take him seriously then he'd have to try again, but that was the thing, wasn't it? Trying on a serious love confession would only make things worse, especially having been dished out such a polite rejection as Jacobi had given him in the car.

"Best tamp down on that whole mess, old boy," he told himself fuzzily. "He deserves far better than being pawed at by some fawning idiot of a young master, what?"

Jacobi hadn't given Alphonse his resignation, at least, but he could be waiting for Alphonse to be clear-headed enough to accept it. Normally Alphonse would beg on bended knee for Jacobi to stay, but he couldn't very well do that now, could he? Ask the man to continue in his employ, knowing Alphonse was in love with him? Because Jacobi must know. Alphonse had all but said so, and Jacobi was very good at reading between the lines. It would be terribly awkward to ask him to stay, not to mention inappropriate, and not at all the sort of situation to which Alphonse wanted to contribute. Workplace harassment, and the like. No: if Jacobi wished to resign, Alphonse would let him go without so much as a single plea falling from his lips.

"Chin up, old boy," he told himself, sitting there in the dark, wringing his hands anxiously atop the bedcovers. "What's done is done. All you can do now is move forward and accept the consequences for your actions."

The night, or rather, early morning, slipped ever closer to dawn, and Alphonse, having been abed for the past twelve hours, remained despairingly awake. The blue hour came on, turning the fuzzy darkness of the bedroom rich and deep before the sun peeked over the horizon and the day's first rays of light came pale and grey around the curtains. Finally, at seven, before the light turned properly yellow, Alphonse threw off his covers and rose, determined to face his fate head-on.

The instant he set foot to floor, every agony he had sustained from his fall came slamming into his body, and he barely managed to muffle his groan. He'd been so preoccupied with the damage he might have done to his relationship with Jacobi that he'd clean forgotten the damage done to his body, but now that he was properly conscious, his muscles were quick to remind him. He'd taken a tumble from horseback before in his life, naturally, but not in recent years, and he found the experience so much worse than he remembered. His back was stiff like he'd slept on it in the wrong position, his shoulders the same, and the less said of his rump, the better. Easing himself out of bed, he winced his way across the room to the mirror and shuffled his pyjama bottoms down just low enough to examine the pink and purple bruise sprawled across his posterior.

"Cripes," he whispered. "It's a wonder it didn't hurt more at the time!"

It really was impressive in size and colour both, and though it was awfully sore, he couldn't help but admire it a little. The only thing worse than a bad fall was a bad fall with nothing to show for it, after all.

A footstep like the soft tread of a cat sounded from outside the door, and Alphonse jumped, hurriedly pulling his pyjama bottoms back up over his hips. Of course Jacobi was already up; it was his custom to start the day hours ahead of Alphonse. Seven a.m. might be inhumanely early for Alphonse, but not so for his esteemed counterpart.

"Sir?" The lightest tap at the door, so light that had Alphonse still been abed, it would never have woken him.

"Yes, Jacobi?"

The door eased open and Jacobi appeared, looking as polished as ever.

"I anticipated that you might rise earlier than your norm, sir. Shall I prepare breakfast?"

Alphonse blinked. That didn't sound like an immediate tendering of a resignation. "Yes, breakfast. That sounds like just the thing. Nothing too heavy though, what? I'm absolutely starved, but my stomach's a bit shaky, and I'm not confident I could keep down a proper fry-up. Must be the end of that God's Tongue in my system."

It could very well be the God's Tongue that was making his stomach twist itself in knots, but he suspected it had more to do with nerves. The sight of Jacobi filling his doorway was all he ever wanted, but it had never inspired such awful trepidation before. In every millisecond of silence between them, Alphonse expected Jacobi to politely inform him that as soon as breakfast was over, so too was his employment.

But Jacobi merely inclined his head as he always did at Alphonse's instruction, and shimmered away, presumably to the kitchen to prepare the day's first meal. Alphonse stayed where he was, rooted fast to the floor and quite incapable of unsticking himself. Of all the scenarios he had fearfully imagined the morning would bring, he hadn't expected Jacobi to ignore the previous day's events as if they had never happened.

Perhaps he was waiting to break the news to Alphonse gently, over the meal. It was much too soon for Alphonse to relax and assume that the danger had passed.

"Righto," Alphonse told himself firmly. "If he's not going to mention it, then you're not going to bring it up first. You overstepped enough boundaries yesterday, old chap, so you just sit tight and let him set them today."

Finally unrooting his feet from the floor, Alphonse strode to his wardrobe and pulled out the first suit he landed on, determined to get himself dressed before Jacobi returned. He remembered all too clearly the torture of letting Jacobi change him into his pyjamas the previous afternoon, and refused to subject himself to any such thing again. The memory was simply unbearable, especially knowing that it was likely the last time Jacobi would ever touch him in such a manner. He must have done it out of a misplaced sense of duty. Alphonse couldn't bear to think that Jacobi had done it out of pity; the idea caused a sharp pang in his chest and a new knot to form in his stomach. No: it came from a need to help his incapacitated master who had clearly lost his wits under the influence of a foreign drug. But now that Alphonse had regained his sobriety, Jacobi had no need to attend to him so closely, especially not now that he knew the depth of Alphonse's feelings for him. Feelings that, if their exchange in the car was anything to go by, were unreciprocated.

Straightening his tie in the mirror, Alphonse looked up and came face to face with a young man who looked so helplessly lost that he nearly gave it all up and went straight back to bed.

"Buck up," he told himself, somewhat desperately.

If he went back to bed it would only concern Jacobi and cause the man to play nursemaid to him again, which was surely the last thing Jacobi wanted. So, steeling himself, Alphonse forced himself out of the bedroom and into the kitchen, putting a spring in his step even if he couldn't convince his face to hold a cheerful expression.

"Tea and toast, sir, with a plate of fruit on the side. I imagine you'll regain your appetite in another hour or two, and you might be interested in taking a fuller breakfast at that time."

Alphonse slid into his chair at the kitchen table and immediately shoved a slice of apple into his mouth to stall for time, wincing as the sour juice did nothing to settle his stomach. "Jolly good," he said around the fruit. "Looks delicious, I must say. Maybe I'll replace the classic fry-up with something like this more often, what do you say?"

"I'm delighted you find it to your satisfaction, sir. How are you feeling this morning, other than your stomach? Are you experiencing any other after-effects from the drug?"

That was an invitation, Alphonse realised, to take back everything he had said the day before. He could so easily wave it all aside as being the madcap ramblings of a drugged mind, deny every lovesick confession he had made, both spoken and unspoken, and wipe the slate clean between them. He could set Jacobi's mind at ease and ensure that the man had no reason to find some other, better employer.

But he could only do that at the cost of swallowing his own feelings.

"I feel much better," Alphonse hedged, fiddling with the fruit platter. "I can keep my legs under me again, which is a great improvement, I'm sure you agree. And my thoughts are much easier to organise than they were, all lined up one after another the way they should be, with much less risk of any slipping out unattended."

He chanced a glance up at Jacobi to gauge his reaction, but Jacobi, occupied with washing up the knife and cutting board from his fruit-cutting endeavour, merely raised one eyebrow without looking over and uttered a neutral, "Indeed, sir?"

That didn't give Alphonse much to work with. "Indeed, indeed. I'd even go so far as to say that my brain feels scrubbed clean like someone went at it with a scouring pad overnight, and I've woken up all shiny and refreshed."

"I'm glad to hear it, sir."

"In fact," Alphonse continued, growing increasingly desperate for Jacobi to give him some meaningful input, "I feel so capable and rejuvenated that you might as well take the day off. I thought to spend mine at the Stag's Head: the whole day, from start to finish. Maybe I'll even have dinner there. Who knows? I've never had quite so much day spread out before me; I hardly know what to do with all of it. What do people do when they get up so early in the morning?"

"Most of them have jobs and responsibilities, I imagine, sir."

"Oh, pish. I haven't got any of those—and neither have you for the rest of the day, if you don't want them. The world is your oyster as much as it is mine, and I say we make the most of it. Separately, I mean," he added hastily. "I don't imagine you want to spend your day with me at the club. You've got far better taste than that, and I'm sure you've got all manner of things to attend to in your personal life that don't involve me one bit. As you should! So I'll just hare off and get out from under your feet and leave you to it. Doing whatever it is you need to get done. Or not doing anything at all! Think of it as a mini vacation. You're long overdue for some time off, I think."

"I have most nights and weekends off, sir," Jacobi pointed out in a tone of gentle bemusement.

"And now you've got today off, too!" Crunching through the end of his toast, Alphonse shoved one last handful of fruit into his mouth as he rose from the table in a clatter and made a beeline for the exit. "Don't expect me back for dinner. Don't expect me back at all! I'll turn up at some point, and I'm sure we'll run into each other naturally, as people do. Toodles!"

And then he all but fled the flat, not daring to look back and see Jacobi's expression.

♦ ♦ ♦

The Stag's Head was close to abandoned so early in the day, and Alphonse moped about from room to room without having nearly enough company to distract him from his woes. He threw a few darts and had a go at the pool table, but his aim was abysmal in both cases, and there wasn't even anyone around to poke fun at him for it. The library was stuffy and dull, the newspapers vapid, and even he had to allow that it was too early to start drinking. Not that he was much interested in any case: after his misadventure with Aaliyah's God's Tongue, the idea of flinging himself into cheerful oblivion by way of inebriation had no appeal whatsoever.

No: what he needed was a spot of amity. More specifically, he needed a problem-solver. And with Jacobi not being an option, that left Aaliyah, devil though she may be.

He rang her on the club telephone, biting his lip the whole time as he waited for her to pick up.

"Alphonse!" Aaliyah greeted cheerfully once the line connected. "I'm glad you survived the night. How are you holding up?"

"I'm not," he informed her. "I've no idea where I stand with Jacobi, and even less of an idea as to how I'm supposed to figure it out."

"Well, that's a shame. What on earth did you do that could have complicated things so badly?"

"I think he knows I'm in love with him. I was very intent on telling him so yesterday, and I'm afraid he wasn't receptive to that idea at all. And now that it's the morning and I've sobered up again, he seems to be pretending that the conversation never occurred in the first place. And I simply don't know what to do!"

"Did you expect him to broach the subject? Did you even indicate that you remember yesterday's events?"

"Er." Alphonse gnawed on his lip. "Not as such, no. I was looking to him for clues! But he didn't give me so much as a hint, and I'm altogether in the dark."

"For heaven's sake, Alphonse, of course he's going to be wary of you! You were obviously under the influence, insisting that nothing you said was to be taken seriously, while spouting off about your feelings for the man which you'd never mentioned before, nor given any indication of, and then spent the next morning avoiding the subject. Lovestruck ramblings are never to be taken seriously when the speaker is inebriated. I'll bet you anything that your man is waiting for you to sober up and either confirm or deny your feelings with a clear head before he decides how to react. Which is a perfectly sensible way of doing things, by the way. He's following your lead. So, if you want to have a conversation about the matter like an adult, you have to bring it up yourself."

"But isn't that terribly awkward? Inappropriate, I mean."

"A bit, but that ship has already sailed. Besides which, surely it's better to instigate a mildly inappropriate conversation than drag on like this. Someone needs to put you both out of your misery."

"Do you think I'm making him miserable?" Alphonse worried.

"Alphonse," Aaliyah said, her voice perfectly pleasant, "if you don't get this resolved, I'm going to throw you in the Thames. I mean this with love, but you are absolutely ridiculous, and I just haven't got the patience for it. God knows how Jacobi puts up with you."

"Jacobi likes my nonsense," Alphonse said feebly.

"He must do. Anyway: perhaps dinner will help?"

Alphonse dragged one hand down his face. "I don't really see how. Me and him, you mean? I was planning to stay out of the flat until I'd figured something out, to be honest. I could probably live at the Stag's Head for a few days before anyone got very concerned about me. There are some chaps who've lived here for entire weeks when they were avoiding something drastic on the home front. I never thought I'd find myself in such a position, but the precedent stands, which is good."

"Don't live at the club; that's miserably depressing. And no: I meant that you should have dinner with me. All four of us, as a matter of fact: you and I, and Jacobi and Miss Bailey. I think it's high time we all sat down, got to know each other, and hashed out a plan about what to do after the wedding."

"The wedding!" Alphonse groaned. What had once been the greatest and most insurmountable problem in his life had somehow been pushed to the back of his mind over the course of the last day. "Yes, alright, I suppose we'd better. But it's going to be mightily awkward between Jacobi and myself, I can tell you that right now."

"I'm sure you'll work things out. And if you can't smooth things over by this evening, then I'll do my best to provide a buffer while we're all together, seeing as it's partially my fault."

"It's entirely your fault!" Alphonse countered, though he knew that wasn't really true. Even if she hadn't brought his feelings to the surface in such a sudden and dramatic manner, they still would have been simmering away down there, waiting for some other inopportune moment to burst free. It was inevitable.

"Chin up, Hollyhock. I'm sure things will turn out alright in the end."

"And if they don't?" he asked despairingly.

"Then it's not yet the end," she replied, like it was as simple as that.

♦ ♦ ♦

Alphonse slunk back to Portman Square with his tail tucked firmly between his legs, head down and feeling every inch the embarrassed spaniel crawling home to flop at its master's feet. Perhaps by some stroke of luck Jacobi had gone out as Alphonse had suggested, and Aaliyah's dinner plans would be forcibly postponed. But Alphonse's life was doomed to complications, and Jacobi appeared in the living room, unjacketed, with a book in hand.

"Sir? I take it your plans for the day have changed?"

"I don't know why either of us are surprised. My plans rarely go according to—well, to plan."

Alphonse cleared his throat and tipped his head back to regard the ceiling, trying to avoid ogling Jacobi's waist-coated form. He had his shirtsleeves rolled to the elbow, and the sight of his forearms—corded with rippling tendons and dusted with dark hair—flooded Alphonse with unmanageable heat.

"Aaliyah is arranging dinner and wants us both in attendance. If you're really taking the day off then of course you're not obliged to join us, but—"

"Is it to discuss the marriage arrangements, sir? If so, I feel that I should attend."

Alphonse drooped. "Righto. That's our evening set, then. By the way," he added, straightening, "would you remind me who Miss Bailey is? Aaliyah said that there were to be four of us, and I'll cop that the name sounds familiar, but I can't for the life of me place it."

"You met Miss Bailey briefly at Kew Gardens, sir. She was the young woman of Jamaican descent who was accompanying Miss Kaddour before your arrival."

"Ah! The girl you went off with while Aaliyah and I had our talk in the glasshouse. Well. That's. That's lovely, isn't it?"

"She owns a flower-selling business here in London, and I understand she's something of an artist, as well. We shared an illuminating conversation, and she was very pleasant company. I believe, sir, that when you meet her properly over dinner, you will feel the same."

"Oh, I'm sure! Pleasant company all around, the four of us. I can hardly wait." Alphonse swallowed around the lump in his throat. "And it will be nice for you to get the chance to see her again, what? Ever so glad that I had the opportunity to facilitate it." God, why couldn't he stop talking?

"I think you misunderstand the situation, sir," Jacobi said slowly. "Miss Bailey is as attached to Miss Kaddour's side as I am to yours, and we have no intention of pursuing anything like a romantic entanglement."

"No, and why should you?" Alphonse hastily agreed. "You've said before that you don't see yourself settling down, so why bring romance into every single relationship? Both parties can be perfectly satisfied without it, after all. It's an old-fashioned notion anyway, romance. Being in love. Who needs it, am I right?"

Jacobi stared at him for three full seconds before raising one hand and pinching the bridge of his nose, shutting his eyes as if pained by a sudden and terrible headache. Alphonse was taken aback, having never seen such a strong display of emotion from the man, and hardly knew what to say.

"Are you quite alright, old thing?" he ventured.

"Yes, sir. I forget sometimes the way in which you move through the world. You must forgive me."

"What way is that?"

Jacobi dropped his hand, though the pained expression had not entirely left his face. "Obliviously, sir."

"That's accurate. In any case: shall I tell Aaliyah that dinner is on for tonight? She suggested that I host the affair, as insurance against any event in which I panic and try to run away. I told her I was amenable, of course, but that I'd have to check with you, seeing as you're the one who'd be playing chef for the night."

"I don't mind cooking for four, but I'll have to collect groceries beforehand. Do Miss Kaddour or Miss Bailey have any dietary preferences that you know of, sir?"

"I haven't the foggiest. You'll just have to go ahead and use your best judgement, as you always do."

"Very good, sir. Before I go, is there anything else you would like to discuss?"

Alphonse floundered. Jacobi's words were too pointed for Alphonse to evade the question; for once, he knew exactly what the man was driving at. It was the only thing on his mind, after all. Jacobi looked at him evenly, and Alphonse felt his ears go red.

"You weren't at all keen on discussing it yesterday," he mumbled.

"When you were operating under the influence, no, sir, I was not. I thought it kinder to remove myself from the situation and offer you some privacy until you were back in your right mind. To protect your dignity, as it were."

Alphonse sniffed. "My dignity. That's a lost cause and we both know it."

"Sir."

Alphonse shut his mouth.

"Yesterday, you instructed me to disregard every word you said as being inebriated nonsense that couldn't be trusted. Is there anything you were trying to tell me then that you would like to repeat now, knowing I will take you seriously?"

Alphonse swallowed, bolstered his courage, and said, "I want to apologise. You've every right in the world to be upset with me, what with my overstepping of boundaries left and right yesterday. And I'm terribly sorry for it. I blame the drug, naturally, but it's me who's ultimately responsible. It's a rummy business all around."

"As you say, sir, drugs like those have quite a transformative effect on the mind. I don't hold you responsible for your actions yesterday, but your apology is appreciated all the same."

"Then you're not going to resign?" Alphonse asked, wringing his hands together.

"I hadn't planned to, sir. Unless you would like me to leave your service?"

"No!" Alphonse yelped in a panic. "No, absolutely not, I wouldn't like you to leave my service one bit. I just want us to go on as we were before. I did—I do— have feelings for you." He forced himself to meet Jacobi's eye, the man's expression unreadable. "Only recently realised, you see. But I never intended to share them with you, and I certainly don't intend to act on them. I know this makes for a drattedly uncomfortable situation, but if it's not enough for you to resign, then I promise…" He wiped his sweating palms down the sides of his trouser legs and drew a shaky breath. "I promise, nothing will ever come of it. I'll just bottle all this stuff up, and it'll be like I never had a single feeling at all. What?"

"I see," Jacobi said. "Sir, if I may—"

"Anything," Alphonse said quickly.

"These feelings. Do you mean of a sexual nature, sir?"

Mortified, Alphonse meeped, and flushed so hot he thought he might pass out.

"…Or romantic, sir?"

Alphonse's gaze fell to Jacobi's lips before he dragged his eyes back up again, horrified at his lack of control, and clapped one hand over his mouth to keep from blurting out his undying love for the man.

"I see," Jacobi repeated, his eyes warm. "Please be assured, sir: this development will not affect my continued employment. And, should you ever wish to unbottle those feelings and have a more in-depth discussion about them rather than fleeing to the Stag's Head to avoid me…"

Alphonse stared, flabbergasted, his heart rabbiting in his chest.

"Please do take that liberty," Jacobi finished serenely. Then, bowing his head, he said, "Now, unless there is anything else, I'll fetch those groceries for dinner, sir."

Alphonse nodded dumbly, not entirely sure what had just happened, and watched as Jacobi swept from the room.

CHAPTER NINE

THE DINNER PARTY, OR, A MEETING OF MINDS

Alphonse spent the afternoon on tenterhooks, too cautious around Jacobi to get in the way as he normally would, and too embarrassed to go haring off to the Stag's Head again. He paced the living room as Jacobi steamed rice in the kitchen; he reorganised his wardrobe from top to bottom while Jacobi seasoned chicken for a curry, and then he took all his clothes out and reorganised them again. He tried to read a book, and failed. He tried to closet himself away on the balcony in the hopes that the fresh air would clear his mind, and failed in that, too. Finally, having changed his outfit three times and unable to stomach a fourth, he propped himself up in the kitchen doorway to watch Jacobi work. The mouth-watering scent of coconut milk wafted through the air, mingling with the hot bite of exotic spices.

Alphonse's heart beat triple time as sweat beaded on his palms and his breaths came shallowly, like he was standing at the edge of a sheer drop, trying to work up the nerve to fling himself off. Whether he would fall or fly, he couldn't say. In any case, Jacobi's invitation to talk had been genuine, Alphonse was sure. Though Jacobi often said things he didn't mean, they were always couched in enough sarcasm to make his real opinion obvious. And generally, those sarcastic statements were reserved for Alphonse's more questionable fashion choices, and not any kind of serious matter. Jacobi was many things, but never cruel. Alphonse wanted desperately to step into the kitchen and take him by the hands and ask, "If I throw myself off the edge of this cliff, am I going to grow wings or not, and would you please tell me before I commit to it?"

That imaginary Jacobi clasped Alphonse's hands in return, his skin silky and dry compared to the sweaty mess that was Alphonse. He looked deep into Alphonse's eyes, his expression calm and infinitely patient. "Sir, it hardly matters. I'll catch you in any case."

Alphonse smothered his groan behind one hand. It wasn't fair that Jacobi should be so perfect, even in Alphonse's imagination. It was like those blasted cottage dreams all over again.

Before he could enter the kitchen and put that question to Jacobi in the real world, a commotion at the door announced Aaliyah's and Miss Bailey's arrival. Grateful for the distraction, Alphonse rushed to answer the knocking. Pulling open the door, he wrestled a smile onto his face in time for Aaliyah to swoop in and give him a friendly peck on the cheek, carrying a white pastry box tucked under one arm.

"Alright?" she asked in a low voice in his ear.

"I don't know," he hissed back.

"Well, you haven't run off again, so that's something." Drawing back, she raised her voice to a more conversational tone. "You remember Jasmine, don't you? You didn't get the chance to talk before, but—"

"Miss Bailey, yes! So good to meet you properly." Alphonse greeted Aaliyah's companion with a handshake.

"Jasmine, please," Miss Bailey replied. She was a stunningly pretty girl of Alphonse's height, with a wide white smile that looked absolutely dazzling against the dark, rich brown of her skin. The faintest hint of Jamaica coloured her words, but, like Aaliyah, her accent was primarily of south London. "Aaliyah has told me all about you, of course. I look forward to getting to know you better. You and Jacobi both," she added, glancing over Alphonse's shoulder to catch Jacobi's eye in the background.

"Well, if the things you've heard haven't put you off yet, I hope tonight won't. Come in, come in. I'll take your hats and coats. Normally Jacobi does all the butlery things, but he's busy, and he's off duty tonight, besides. Except for cooking."

Once the girls had piled their coats and hats into his arms, Alphonse spun around in a tight circle, trying to figure out where to deposit them until Jacobi cleared his throat from the kitchen and nodded to the coat closet, one eloquent eyebrow raised.

"Ah! Right you are," Alphonse said, relieved at the quick rescue.

Without her coat, Aaliyah was in a sparkling gold dress that seemed more suited to a night on the town than a private dinner party, but Alphonse got the sense that she was always dressed to the nines, regardless of the occasion. Jasmine seemed less inclined to the sequin-and-bead flair of her partner, though she was no duller for it, wearing a bright green dress patterned with yellow flowers like she was headed to a summer garden party after dinner.

Aaliyah flitted straight for the kitchen like she already knew her way around the place, depositing the pastry box on the counter out of Jacobi's way. "I brought dessert," she announced, "and Jasmine brought wine."

"Red and white," Jasmine said, handing Alphonse a tall, narrow bag which did indeed house two bottles. "I didn't know what Jacobi was making, so I brought one of each."

"Spiffing," Alphonse said, trotting to the kitchen to put the wine with Aaliyah's desserts.

"I took inspiration from the Caribbean for tonight's meal," Jacobi said from his place by the stove, where dinner was simmering away and filling the flat with the most delectable array of aromas. "Miss Bailey had mentioned during our previous meeting that she was fond of her country's traditional cuisine, so I've prepared something in that vein."

"White wine, then," Jasmine said confidently, lingering in the kitchen doorway.

Addressing Aaliyah, Jacobi added, "Had I had more time to prepare, I would have looked into some North African cooking for you. But with so little notice, I felt obliged to rely on those recipes with which I already had some passing familiarity."

"I've never been scolded so passive-aggressively in my life," Aaliyah said cheerfully. "You're a saint for putting this together on short notice, and I won't ask you to do it again. And I love Jamaican food, as it happens."

"I fear this is unlikely to meet the standards of authentic Caribbean cuisine," Jacobi demurred, the very picture of modesty.

"I've never had Jamaican food before," Alphonse commented.

"It smells delicious," Jasmine said.

"I've made curried chicken, rice with red beans cooked in coconut milk, and savoury fried plantains on the side." Jacobi turned, scrutinising the clutter of dishes on the stovetop. "And everything will be ready momentarily if you would care to take your places at the dining table."

Alphonse automatically turned towards the dining room, but Aaliyah stopped him short with one hand on his arm.

"Oh, you're not going to serve us, Jacobi!" she said. "The four of us are here as equals tonight, and since you did the cooking, it's only right that you be exempt from everything else."

That made immense sense to Alphonse. "Righto! Shall I serve, then?"

"If you absolutely feel you must, sir."

"I think we're all perfectly capable of serving ourselves," Jasmine said, stepping in diplomatically.

It was only after the four of them had piled their plates high and were relocating to the dining room that Alphonse realised that his long-held fantasy of eating dinner with Jacobi, the two of them sitting down together at the same table, was finally happening. He could barely hold back his smile as they took their seats, he and Jacobi side by side across from Aaliyah and Jasmine, the heads of the table left empty. As they were all getting settled, Aaliyah caught Alphonse's eye and gave him a significant look, nodding imperceptibly towards Jacobi.

"All good?" she asked, as if checking that everyone was comfortable.

"I'm optimistic," he said tentatively. "About the food," he added hastily, looking to Jacobi to ensure that the man hadn't picked up on the undercurrent of their conversation. "Which I'm sure will be excellent, of course."

"Thank you, sir."

"I don't think you have anything to worry about," Aaliyah said.

"You keep saying that," Alphonse muttered, but thought for the first time that maybe she was right.

Rather than squabble about it right under Jacobi's nose, he poured the dry, fruity white wine that Jasmine had supplied, and when everyone's cups were full, Aaliyah raised her glass in a toast.

"To new beginnings," she declared.

"And new friends," Jasmine added.

Jacobi raised his glass silently, but his knee nudged Alphonse's under the table, and Alphonse had a small conniption trying to work out whether it was intentional. Jacobi's face gave nothing away, so Alphonse lifted his glass and said, "Here, here!" And then took rather too large a gulp of the stuff to keep from asking Jacobi what he meant by it, and why he had yet to move his knee away.

Toast made, they wasted no more time with formalities before taking up their forks and digging in. The food was every bit as delicious as it smelled: the chicken curry swimming with green vegetables, the meat tender, and all of it doused in the spiciest orange sauce that Alphonse had ever tasted. The rice and red beans were so soft they practically melted in his mouth, the coconut milk a welcome relief from the heat of the curry, and the fried plantains were just sweet enough to keep him coming back for more. He was the only one at the table who seemed ill-equipped to handle the spice, his eyes streaming as he kept opening his mouth to pant in between bites, trying to cool his burning tongue.

"Is this considered very spicy by English standards?" Jasmine asked Jacobi in an aside.

"Unfortunately, yes," Aaliyah replied.

"I do apologise, sir," Jacobi said to Alphonse. "I was trying to compromise between your palate and the spices inherent in Caribbean food, but I see I've overshot the mark."

"It's fine," Alphonse assured him, openly weeping into his plate. "It's good! I'll adapt." He coughed weakly before shovelling a forkful of rice into his mouth, desperate for the coconut to bring some respite.

"The food is excellent, Jacobi, but the heat is really nothing," Aaliyah said. "I think Alphonse is just delicate."

"Yes, I am, rather." Alphonse swallowed another mouthful of wine. "Mockery well deserved and all that, but let's ease me into the spicier side of things, what? Give me a chance to get my feet under me before throwing me in the deep end."

"This is the shallowest possible end there is. This is barely deep enough to dip your toe in, compared to the ocean of spice available."

"The whole marriage is going to go like this, isn't it?" Alphonse asked mournfully.

"Yes," Aaliyah said, and topped up his glass, finishing the bottle. "Speaking of, let's get down to business, shall we? We have far too much to discuss to waste the whole evening on small talk. Alphonse, have you got any particularly strong opinions about how you want your wedding to unfold?"

"My only preference is that it should be as painless as possible."

"In that case, you'll want to stay away from the planning stage altogether. That's fine; I like being in charge of things. Provided your mother and I can agree on a few key details, I'm confident we can have it all hashed out within a week. All you'll have to do is choose your groomsmen and meet my father at some point before the big day. Not now," she added in the face of Alphonse's panic. "He's overseas on business at the moment, but he'll be back in order to walk me down the aisle next summer. I'm sure he'll like you well enough. He's very good about trusting my judgement in these matters. Other than that, you just have to show up on time and let it happen."

"Stand at the altar and look pretty? I can do that."

"Good. Now, as for the matter of rings." Aaliyah took Jasmine's hand, linking their fingers. Jasmine switched her fork to her other hand and continued eating. "I'd like Jasmine to choose my engagement ring, unless you have any objection to that." Her expression advised Alphonse that an objection would be a very bad thing to have, as if he actually needed the warning.

"Jolly good! I don't know the first thing about rings anyway. It's a considerable relief, really, to have someone else take care of all that. We'll just say I picked it out, what?"

"Exactly. And as for wedding rings, I thought to do the same."

"Oh, but I'll need to wear a wedding band as well. Should Jasmine pick mine out too, so they'll be a matching set?"

"Actually, I thought Jacobi might select yours," Aaliyah said lightly.

"I don't feel we know each other well enough to choose a ring for you," Jasmine explained.

"Jacobi chooses everything else for you," Aaliyah continued, "and his fashion sense is very tasteful. I'm sure he'll find you the perfect thing."

"I— Well," Alphonse stammered, looking to Jacobi for direction as a flush heated his cheeks. Their legs were still pressed together under the table, which wasn't helping matters in the least. "If you want to, then yes, I'd be happy to have you choose my ring."

"Certainly, sir. Perhaps Miss Bailey and I should go together, to ensure our choices complement one another."

Jasmine broke into a smile as she squeezed Aaliyah's fingers on top of the table. "I'd be delighted. We'll make a day of it."

"Righto," Alphonse said.

Something that had been niggling in the back of his mind since the hunt made its way to the forefront. He chewed it over for a few minutes while the others chatted, growing increasingly nervous, until there came a brief lull in the conversation, and he jumped back in.

"Do you really prefer Algeria to England?" he asked Aaliyah. Jacobi and Jasmine glanced back and forth between the two of them, Jasmine looking like she already knew the answer, and Jacobi curious. "Five years into marriage, are you going to decide you're sick of it here and whisk me off to Africa? Because I'm not opposed to a bit of travel and sight-seeing, but I'd always intended to live out my life in London. I suppose we could do a long-distance relationship, only I'm not sure how our families would like that."

Aaliyah set her fork down, affording Alphonse her full attention. "I've lived in England since I was five. I hardly remember Algiers, to be honest. I'd like to return someday, if only to visit, but I have no intention of transplanting you to another continent."

His nervousness dissipated in the face of her no-nonsense reply. "Oh. Jolly good, then."

"When my parents immigrated, they were intent on raising me English. They embraced the culture wholeheartedly: language and religion and almost everything else. I only have the barest ties to Algeria or Islam, to my chagrin. It's just that when people ask about my home, expecting me to drop to my knees in gratitude at being allowed to live in a place as wonderfully perfect as England— Well, I can't stand the presumption. Someone has to stick up for the Barbary Coast, and it might as well be me." She paused. "Fuck the French, though."

"And the British," Jasmine added serenely, clinking her glass against Aaliyah's.

"Anyone you'd like to add to the list?" Alphonse asked Jacobi.

"I'd best not, sir. It runs the risk of quickly getting out of hand."

THE BACHELOR'S VALET

"Fair enough," Alphonse agreed. To Aaliyah, he asked, "Do you miss it? Algerian culture?"

"I still speak French and Arabic with my family, so that's something. And we still cook all the old family recipes. As for the rest?" She shrugged. "I don't know. It's just something I have to feel out as I go along."

Jasmine leaned over to press their shoulders together, a silent show of solidarity. Alphonse made a mental note to study a world map, or perhaps an encyclopedia, in case either of them ever wanted to have a real conversation with him on the topic of their homelands. He didn't own either item, but was confident that Jacobi could roust something up for him.

In the meantime, he said, "And Jasmine, you're not keen on haring off back to Jamaica and taking Aaliyah with you?"

Jasmine shook her head, draining the last of her wine. "My mother immigrated here when I was very small. I'd like to visit someday, but that's a distant dream. My business is here."

"Excellent! And Jacobi—"

"Has no intention of removing you from London, sir."

"Good, good. Relieving news all around!"

"We will have to remove you from this flat, though," Aaliyah said. "There's just no way for all four of us to live here. We're going to need a proper house."

"I've already begun looking into the matter," Jacobi said.

"Have you? When?" Alphonse asked.

"As soon as you proposed, sir. Purchasing a house seemed inevitable if you were to marry, so I saw no sense in putting it off."

"I've done a little light house-hunting myself," Aaliyah said. "We'll have to compare notes."

"And you're sure no one will question the four of us moving in together?" Alphonse asked, toying with the stem of his wine glass. "I know you explained it to me before, but you can't deny it's a little unusual, four grown adults shacking up."

"It's a touch unusual," Aaliyah granted, "but personally, I'm not worried whatsoever. To anyone on the outside looking in, we're going to seem like a perfectly in-love young married couple who have enough money to keep our hired help within arm's reach at all times."

"Isn't that a bit inappropriate, though? Hiring Jasmine on as your assistant at the same time as pursuing an intimate relationship?"

"I'm only pretending to hire her," Aaliyah countered. "It's all a front to keep people from asking questions."

"I'll continue running my business quite separately from my personal affairs," Jasmine said. "I'll pretend to be Aaliyah's assistant when we're in mixed company, but in private, as we are now, I will act nothing of the sort."

Aaliyah turned a winsome grin in her direction. "And I wouldn't want you to."

"Are you not going to hire any servants at all, then?" Alphonse asked curiously.

"I'm quite capable of running my own life and my own house. I don't see the necessity of adding a fifth person to our little party so long as we all pull our own weight."

"To be clear: we don't expect Jacobi to pick up two extra people's-worth of serving duties?"

"We do not," Jacobi said, in a tone that left no room for argument.

"We absolutely don't," Aaliyah confirmed. And then, without regard for Alphonse's poor nerves, went on to say, "Whatever relationship you two choose to pursue is your own business. If he stays on as your valet then I don't expect him to pick up after me, and if you end up in an arrangement like Jasmine and I have, then I certainly don't expect him to perform any more duties than the rest of us. As far as I'm concerned, that's something for the two of you to work out between yourselves."

"Oh," Alphonse stuttered, "I don't think—"

"I agree," Jacobi cut in, not seeming remotely alarmed by Aaliyah's suggestion that he and Alphonse might end up somehow intimate. "And of course, whatever situation should arise, I'm capable of enforcing my own boundaries."

Aaliyah smiled and reached across the table to pat his hand in a supportive, or perhaps co-conspiratorial, way. "As long as you don't ever feel like you're being taken advantage of," she said sweetly.

"Thank you, Miss Kaddour. But I believe I can hold my own."

"You're not being taken advantage of, are you?" Alphonse asked anxiously.

"Not that I know of, sir."

"That's that settled, then," Aaliyah said. "Now, is there any more business to get out of the way, or shall we move on to dessert?"

"Dessert, please," Alphonse voted.

Aaliyah rose from her chair in a flash of beads and sequins, darting into the kitchen to retrieve her pastry box. Alphonse followed her to snag a white dessert wine from the cabinet, and they all relocated to the living room for the remainder of the evening. Alphonse and Jacobi took up their armchairs while Aaliyah and Jasmine claimed the sofa. Setting the pastry box on the coffee table that stood central in the room, equidistant from each seat, Aaliyah opened it to reveal a cluster of sweets, each one nestled in a paper doily. The desserts were triangular in shape, some yellow, some pink, and others white, all of them decorated with intricate swirls of icing. Alphonse couldn't put a name to them, but they looked delicious, and his mouth flooded with water at the first scent.

"These are mkhabez; I hope you like almonds. I have lemon, rosewater, and vanilla."

"They look scrumptious," Alphonse said, pulling his chair in to give them a closer look. "What did you call them? Mkhabez?"

"They're a traditional Algerian dessert. My grandmother taught me how to make them."

"Aaliyah baked these herself," Jasmine said proudly.

THE BACHELOR'S VALET

"So I'd better appreciate them, you mean." Alphonse dipped into the box to snag a yellow one. "Lemon, is it?"

Jacobi selected a vanilla, Jasmine a pink rosewater one, and Aaliyah shrugged before taking one of each, stacking them up on her plate like a pyramid.

"They're small," she pointed out. "I'm taking all of mine at once in case you go back for seconds, and end up fighting over the choices."

"I'm sure we won't," Alphonse protested, then took a bite and immediately reconsidered that stance. It was so good that he might have to fight off everyone else to get his hands on more. The taste was sweet, the sharp zing of the lemon cutting through the earthy taste of ground almonds, the citrus making his mouth water and the sugar tempting him to go back in for an immediate second helping.

"These are amazing," he said with his mouth full, manners be damned. "I hope you'll make them again after we're married."

"You haven't even finished your first one," Aaliyah retorted, eating her own much more daintily, though she seemed pleased by the compliment.

Alphonse cracked open the dessert wine as the conversation meandered from one easy topic to the next. As the evening wore on, the food and company lulled Alphonse into a state of relaxation, his limbs growing heavier as he melted into his chair. When Aaliyah stole a fourth pastry from the box, Alphonse hurriedly grabbed one of each of the two flavours he had yet to try before they all disappeared, before remembering to be a good host and distributing the remaining pastries between Jacobi and Jasmine.

As he leaned over to give Jacobi his share, the man caught his arm and said, "Wait. You have something…"

Alphonse held perfectly still as Jacobi reached up and touched the corner of Alphonse's mouth, thumb brushing his lips and lingering there for a second before pulling away.

"A crumb," Jacobi said.

"Thank you," Alphonse said faintly, collapsing back into his chair with one hand raised to his mouth, echoing Jacobi's touch. His lips tingled from the memory and his stomach flipped delightedly, and not just from the wine.

Once the pastries were gone, the dessert wine quickly followed, prompting him to fetch Jasmine's bottle of red. Ten o'clock rolled around to find everyone pleasantly tipsy, and then eleven o'clock appeared seemingly within minutes. It was close to midnight when Jasmine and Aaliyah finally announced that they should head off, and Alphonse was startled to note the late hour.

"I'm sure we'll do this again sometime soon," Aaliyah said, donning her hat and coat.

"As long as you bring more of those desserts, we can do this as often as you like," Alphonse invited.

"I'll cook next time," Jasmine offered, "though I must warn you that tonight's spices are nothing compared to mine."

"Oh, that's alright. I'll supply the wine. If I get tipsy enough, maybe I won't notice that my face is burning off."

Aaliyah leaned in to give Alphonse a quick embrace, pecking his cheek before turning on Jacobi to do the same. Jacobi held himself rigidly in her arms, not moving a muscle until she retreated with a laugh, one hand on his chest. "Sorry. We'll work to up to that." Whirling away and sliding one arm around Jasmine's waist, she added, "Maybe you can practice with Alphonse. Good night!"

"Good night," Jasmine said, offering them each a smile in turn as Aaliyah pulled the door open.

"Night," Alphonse echoed. "See you soon!"

"Good night," Jacobi said, stepping forward to catch the door and shut it behind them as they skipped from the flat, arms around each other like they were two halves of the same soul.

As he shut the door and turned the latch, silence fell for the first time in hours, and Alphonse and Jacobi were alone together once more.

CHAPTER TEN

THE NECESSARY INTIMACIES INHERENT IN BATHTIME

"That went well," Alphonse said with tentative optimism, leaning into a mighty stretch, his arms crossed above his head as he tried to work the cricks out of his back. He was awfully sore, the whole of the past twenty-four hours crashing into him at once, and it seemed unlikely that he would be able to stretch that soreness out, no matter how loose the alcohol had left him.

"I think it did, sir," Jacobi agreed, moving to clear the plates and glasses away from the coffee table.

"Oh, don't bother with any of that. It's not right for you to do any work, not after you've had dinner and drinks sitting down with the rest of us."

"I'll be the one cleaning up in the morning if I don't do it now, sir," Jacobi pointed out, not pausing. "Unless you would like to do the tidying up."

"I will, if it means you taking a load off," Alphonse challenged, even though he didn't know the first thing about cleaning, and Jacobi was well aware of that fact.

Jacobi cast him an amused look but didn't reply, ferrying the last of the used dishes into the kitchen sink before returning to the living room and reclaiming his seat. Alphonse beamed at the apparent compromise and dropped back into his own chair, only to groan at the impact his bottom made with the cushions, having once again forgotten his bruises.

"If I may suggest, sir: a hot bath might relieve the worst of your aches before you go to bed tonight."

Alphonse perked up at the idea. "I like the sound of that. I haven't had a proper soak in ages."

"I would have suggested it yesterday afternoon as soon as we got back, but I disliked the thought of leaving you in there unattended, with your state being what it was. But I think now I was remiss in my decision, and should simply have stayed to provide supervision."

"Better late than never," Alphonse declared, trying to ignore the way his heart faltered at the thought of Jacobi tending to him in the bath. He'd have died on the spot if that had happened in the immediate post-hunt, overwhelmed as he had been with newly-realised love. It would be difficult enough to deal with now, even if Jacobi no longer needed to wait around ensuring that he didn't accidentally drown himself in the tub.

"Very good, sir. I'll get the water started."

Jacobi rose and disappeared down the hallway to the bathroom, and Alphonse took the opportunity to pull himself together. Running both hands through his hair and mussing his waves beyond all hope, he pulled in a deep breath and willed his heart to calm. He'd taken hundreds of baths with Jacobi shimmering in and out of the room, and Alphonse had never paid his presence any mind before. It was as natural as the act of bathing itself, having the man by his side at any time of the day or night, in any state of dress or undress.

At least, it had felt perfectly natural before Alphonse's little revelation. Now everything was shivery and uncertain, sending thrills of heat through his core at the most inopportune moments, like he was a hapless youth again. His love was in turns both exciting and embarrassing. Initially mortifying, but that had slowly worn away over the course of the dinner, as he and Jacobi had regained their footing with one another, and Jacobi seemed altogether disinclined to leave him. Alphonse felt like he was falling in love for the first time all over again. In fact, it felt better than the first time he had been in love, because Jacobi outmatched Featherstrop in every possible way.

Well, every way but one. Featherstrop might be a bit of an idiot, and he might be a bit careless with other people's hearts, but he wasn't Alphonse's valet, and

Alphonse had never got the sense of there being anything inappropriate about their match.

But if the mood from dinnertime was anything to go by, maybe things would turn out alright after all. Aaliyah seemed confident that they would, anyway, and she had been right about everything else so far.

"If I have to put my trust in somebody," he declared to the room at large, "then it might as well be my fiancée."

"I'm glad to hear it, sir," Jacobi said, returning. "She seems a remarkably bright young lady, and someone you want as an ally."

"I certainly don't want her as an enemy. I shudder to think of the carnage she could wreck if she were so inclined."

"Indeed." Jacobi dipped his head in agreement. "Your bath is ready, sir."

"Jolly good." With a wincing groan, Alphonse levered himself up from the chair and hobbled his way past Jacobi and down the hall. "Remarkable how quickly a body can go stiff," he commented as he entered the bathroom with Jacobi on his heels. "That God's Tongue must have really knocked the sensation clean out of me yesterday. Even this morning I wasn't as bad as I am now."

"Yes, sir. I imagine you still had some of the drug in your system when you got up," Jacobi replied, holding out one arm in expectation of collecting Alphonse's suit.

Alphonse froze. He had clean forgotten that having a bath meant de-robing as Jacobi stood by. Jacobi always excused himself from the room before Alphonse removed the very last layer of his clothes, but if he had begun his employ by stripping Alphonse to the skin on a regular basis, Alphonse wouldn't have questioned it. Jacobi did everything with a quiet confidence that implied that he knew exactly what he was doing, and as a result, Alphonse had never once hesitated before undressing in his company in all his five years of having his baths run by the man.

"Would you like me to go, sir?" Jacobi asked, his tone perfectly smooth as if nothing were amiss.

"No," Alphonse said slowly. "No, I'm sorry, old thing. The wine caught up to me for a second there, but I'm quite alright."

He removed his jacket, holding it out to Jacobi like an offering. Jacobi folded it neatly over his arm before stepping into Alphonse's space just as he had done the previous night, his hands coming up to Alphonse's neck to loosen the knot of his tie, and then sliding it free from his collar in a single elegant motion. Alphonse held his breath as Jacobi moved to his shirt buttons, undoing them one at a time before pulling the hem loose from his trousers and circling to Alphonse's back to slide the shirt from his shoulders.

"You're quiet this evening, sir."

"I suppose I am."

And he was going to stay quiet, at least until the undressing was over with. He chewed his bottom lip as Jacobi unbuttoned his trousers, tugging them smartly down from his hips before giving Alphonse room to step out of them. When his trousers were folded and

THE BACHELOR'S VALET

added to the stack of discarded clothes, Jacobi dropped to a single knee, and Alphonse almost had an aneurysm right then and there. If Jacobi noticed the tiny strangled sound that escaped Alphonse's throat, he made no mention of it, his infinitely patient attention still fixed on Alphonse's attire as he peeled off Alphonse's socks one at a time. Jacobi's silence was the only thing saving Alphonse from burning up with embarrassment and want. His silence meant that they could still pretend this was a strictly professional arrangement.

But this, they had never done before. Normally, Jacobi's services were limited to the tying of complicated tie knots, or the buttoning and unbuttoning of shirts and jackets when Alphonse was tipsy enough to lose his coordination, or the straightening of suits and removing of imaginary dust specks. Alphonse rested one hand on Jacobi's shoulder to keep his balance, fingertips dancing over the man's suit for a second like a flighty bird before he gathered his courage and committed to the touch. It felt different, touching Jacobi in this scenario compared to all the other hundreds of thousands of times they had touched before. Even when Alphonse had been delirious with love and drugs the previous day, hanging off Jacobi like a spider monkey, that hadn't been charged with the same electric intent that ran between them now, like they were each waiting for the other to make the first move.

Well, Alphonse certainly wasn't going to be the one to do it. Not without Jacobi's express verbal permission first. Until Jacobi said any such thing—if he said anything at all—Alphonse would simply suffer, burning up in the delicious wave of heat that Jacobi inspired with his every look and touch.

When Alphonse had been stripped of every article of clothing save for his underthings, Jacobi stood back, his arms piled high with clothes.

Eyes averted, he said, "I will return momentarily to confirm that the water is to your liking, sir."

And then he slipped out of the bathroom, leaving Alphonse standing alone next to the tub as the steam rose in thick waves, beginning to curl his hair before he even set foot in the water. What would happen if Jacobi returned to find Alphonse still standing there? Alphonse's heart skipped a beat at the thought, but he wasn't bold enough to test it. It seemed too soon. So, he stripped out of his underthings, tossed them onto the chair in the corner without bothering to fold them, as he never bothered to fold anything unless Jacobi was glaring at him from across the room, and tentatively stepped into the tub.

The water was almost hot enough to scald, and Alphonse hissed as he eased himself into it. It felt good, though, an instant balm to his aches and pains, and the steam was perfumed with rose and lavender, encouraging him to sit back and shut his eyes. The sparkling rainbow of bubbling foam that sat atop the water embraced him like a cloud, clinging to any part of his skin not yet submerged.

In fact, the warmth felt so good that he had nearly drifted off by the time Jacobi returned. He announced his presence with a gentle tap against the door, pausing there for a second to ensure that Alphonse had registered it before sweeping into the room. Alphonse straightened up, trying to bring himself back to alertness. He needed to be keen to navigate the rest of the evening with Jacobi, even though he wanted nothing more than to fall into the man's arms and see what happened. Or, seeing as it was late and he was full of wine, he might just go to bed and see what the next day would bring.

Or, ideally, a combination of the two. To go to bed with Jacobi—with nothing sordid in the suggestion, but merely to lay beside him and share a pillow and fall asleep and wake together— The thought made his insides feel as light and fluffy as the bath foam, and he had to swallow it down before it escaped.

"The water's perfect," he said, rather than trying to articulate any of that. "I don't know how you find just the right temperature every time, but you've got a real knack for it."

"Thank you, sir. I do hope it's giving you some relief."

"Very much," Alphonse assured him. "I know it's not a miracle cure or anything, but I really did notice an improvement the instant I got in. A ripping suggestion, as ever."

"I'm glad to hear it, sir. Though I must warn you that your aches will likely persist another day, if past experience is anything to go by."

"Ugh, I expect you're right. But there's nothing to be done about that unless I sit in the bath that whole time, which I don't imagine would be very comfortable.

I'd go all pruney, for one thing, and I don't care for that at all. A dashedly unattractive look if I do say so myself."

"If I may suggest, sir, there are certain measures you may take in addition to a bath that might cut short the worst of your future aches."

"Please do suggest!"

"The first might be to have me wash your hair for you, sir."

Alphonse automatically lifted one hand to touch his own head, inadvertently depositing a fluff of bath foam atop his curls. When he spoke, he had no idea how he managed to keep his voice at all even. "If you like, then yes, by all means. Do save me the trouble of doing it myself."

"Very good, sir."

Jacobi lay a folded towel over the rim of the bathtub by Alphonse's head, and then, to Alphonse's delight and horror, rolled his shirtsleeves up past the elbow and sat down. He produced a pitcher from somewhere, and dipped it into the bathwater before wordlessly encouraging Alphonse to move forward towards the middle of the tub. Alphonse obeyed, skin squeaking against the porcelain, and then went limp as a kitten at the first touch of Jacobi's hand on the back of his neck, lightly holding him in place as he poured the pitcher over Alphonse's head. Bringing both hands up to shield his face as the hot water came rushing down, Alphonse barely resisted the urge to give his head a good shake like a wet dog. Jacobi doused him twice more before setting the pitcher aside and taking up the shampoo.

Turning sideways, Alphonse drew his knees to his chest and pressed his back against the side of the tub where Jacobi sat. Shutting his eyes, he tipped his head back to give Jacobi better access, and the man wasted no time in pouring a dollop of shampoo onto his palms and setting both hands against Alphonse's crown. The first touch was electrifying, and it only got better from there. Jacobi massaged the shampoo into Alphonse's hair, scratching blunt fingernails against his scalp in such a way as to send the most delicious tingles rushing up and down his spine. Shivering, he leaned into it, and Jacobi rewarded him with a low hum of approval, which only made Alphonse melt into him all the more.

"I say, you're awfully good at this, aren't you?"

"Thank you, sir. I think it important to cultivate a repertoire of skills for any occasion, no matter how unlikely it is to arise."

"That's why you're the best," Alphonse informed him hazily. "I'm going to have you do this every time I have a bath now. I hope you don't mind."

"Not at all, sir. It would be my pleasure, I assure you."

Alphonse wanted to turn around to see if Jacobi had that little smile curling in the corner of his mouth, the one he always got when he was particularly amused. It seemed impossible that he should be wearing the same detached focus that he donned whenever he was performing his usual duties. But Alphonse was afraid that if he turned around he might break whatever spell they were under, and besides which, he didn't want Jacobi to stop doing that thing with his hands.

But one can't wash the same head of hair forever, and all too soon, Jacobi was rinsing the suds from Alphonse's scalp, tilting his head in one direction and then the other to ensure that there was no soap hiding anywhere to itch at him later.

"Jolly good," Alphonse said with a contented sigh when he was done. "I've never felt so relaxed in my life." Which was true, but he'd never felt so hot under his skin either, like there was a fire burning low in the pit of his stomach, and Jacobi was his only chance of putting it out—or stoking it higher.

Jacobi was quiet for a moment, not moving from his perch on the edge of the tub, before he asked in a low voice, "Would you like me to continue, sir?"

Alphonse blinked his eyes open. "What, and wash my hair all over again?"

"No, sir."

Jacobi laid his hands on Alphonse's shoulders, skin to skin, and Alphonse's heart stopped dead. But rather than scrub his back as Alphonse had expected, Jacobi kept his hands where they were, radiating heat as he applied gentle pressure, his thumbs pressing into a knot of muscle at the base of Alphonse's neck.

"The best remedy for muscle soreness, sir, is a massage. And though I am by no means a professional, I do think it's within my reach to provide you some relief in this manner. If you would lean forward, sir? And please tell me if I'm going too hard on you."

"Go as hard as you like," Alphonse replied unthinkingly, his brain whited out in shock.

THE BACHELOR'S VALET

He didn't have words to express the sensation of Jacobi's hands on his skin, kneading into sore muscles and seeking out every ounce of tension and stress in his body, some of which he didn't even know he carried. It was heaven—it was torture—and he wrapped his arms around his knees to sink his teeth into one forearm to keep from moaning. Naturally, the effort only caused him to tense up further, and Jacobi gave a soft admonishment from behind him, pausing in his administrations.

"You must relax if this is to work."

"I'm trying," Alphonse protested. "It's a lot more difficult than you'd think."

"Would you like me to stop?"

"Absolutely not! I can relax. I'll relax."

In an effort to make good on his word, Alphonse dropped his arms back into the water and shut his eyes, willing his body to give itself over to Jacobi's touch without any further protest. Seemingly satisfied, Jacobi continued, working his way down Alphonse's spine until his hands were submerged under the water. They roamed dangerously close to an erogenous zone for a second before climbing back up to Alphonse's shoulders where he dug the heels of his palms in hard enough to pull a groan from Alphonse's chest.

"Do that again," Alphonse begged, giving up on any semblance of pride.

Jacobi obliged, working him over until Alphonse was noodle-limp and in danger of slumping all the way into the water. Only when he was incapable of sitting upright any longer did Jacobi stop, his hands still resting firmly on Alphonse's shoulders, wet skin against wet skin.

"I think that will do for now, sir," he murmured. "The water is going cold, and staying in any longer will undo any progress we have made."

"Is it cold?" Alphonse asked blearily. "I hadn't noticed." To the contrary: he felt hot all over, positively ablaze with desire, but too tipsy and wrung out to do anything about it.

Jacobi rose to his feet, fetching an armful of fresh towels before returning to the side of the tub. "Up you get, sir, before you catch a chill."

Alphonse stood, his legs as wobbly as a new-born colt's, and Jacobi promptly engulfed him in a towel, tying it around his middle before wrapping a second around his head in the style of those turbans the girls were making so fashionable at parties. Offering his arm as a crutch, Jacobi helped Alphonse out of the bath so he could stand, barefoot and dripping, on the lush mat in the middle of the room. For a second, they were both fixed in place, Alphonse's hand still resting on Jacobi's arm as Jacobi held his elbow in a show of support. There was no sound but the soft dripping of water falling from Alphonse's body to the floor.

Jacobi's eyes were dark and steady, trained on Alphonse's face. Alphonse's gaze dropped to Jacobi's lips, and he drew a deep breath before taking one shaky step forward to press himself against Jacobi's front, damp skin grazing the fine material of his suit. If he tipped his head up, he would put them face to face. They were already close enough to feel each other's body heat, still joined hand to arm, Alphonse's bare toes nudging Jacobi's socked ones. Alphonse glanced up through his lashes, lips parted in expectation of what should happen next.

Jacobi exhaled slowly and Alphonse caught his breath, heart thundering so wildly that it seemed about to kick its way straight out of his chest.

But Jacobi didn't lean down to kiss him. His grip on Alphonse's elbow tightened momentarily before he took a step back out of Alphonse's space.

"You should get some sleep, sir."

"Oh," Alphonse said, blinking. "I thought…"

"You've had more than a little to drink," Jacobi said gently, still holding his arm. "And so have I, for that matter."

Alphonse swallowed his protest and ducked his head. "Yes, alright." He could be responsible. Releasing Jacobi's arm, he put distance between them. "Good night, Jacobi."

"Sleep well, sir."

CHAPTER ELEVEN

IN WHICH CERTAIN DREAMS ARE FINALLY DISCUSSED

It was after one in the morning when Alphonse crawled into bed, exhausted and strung tight all at once. He didn't think he would be able to sleep at all, distracted as he was by the memory of standing toe to toe with Jacobi, their faces so close that he could feel Jacobi's breath against his skin, yet somehow not close enough to kiss. Alphonse shifted restlessly between the sheets, turning this way and that, trying to calm the hot, shivery feeling zipping over his skin. Finally, the long day and the wine won out, and he dropped into sleep in the midst of berating himself for not being bolder and leaning in to close that gap between them in the bathroom.

He came to in the kitchen of the dream-cottage, standing in the cosy darkness and watching Jacobi tend to the fire in the hearth. Jacobi was down on one knee, but rather than taking up the iron poker that stood to the side of the fireplace, he encouraged the flames to burn brighter and stronger with little sparks of magic that danced from his fingertips.

Entranced, Alphonse drew closer, his body easy and relaxed like he had never fallen off a horse before in his life. Coming up alongside Jacobi, he leaned one shoulder against the mantel and settled in to watch the man's magic jump and dance over the crackling logs. He could feel the awestruck expression on his face, but did nothing to disguise it. He never did, not with Jacobi, and especially not in his little cottage dreams. The few things he was shy about in the waking world seemed safe to express in the cottage, not because Jacobi seemed like a different person so much as it was that the sharp edges of his professionalism had been worn away to leave someone softer and less ineffable.

"I bet you can light the fire on the first try every time, doing it like that. So much more convenient than all that messing about with matches, I must say."

"It takes a little more effort than striking a match," Jacobi said, rising to his feet, "but I find it a more enjoyable process." He turned to face Alphonse, the firelight flickering off his cheekbones and glowing in his eyes. "I didn't expect to see you here tonight."

"I never expect to find myself here," Alphonse admitted. "I hardly know where *here* is. But I'm always glad when I manage to stumble across it. Infinitely more relaxing than any of my other dreams, I can tell you."

"Yes, I imagine it must be."

"It's like everything's quieter here, and it's easier for me to think. Not that it's possible to make it any harder for me," he added ruefully. "Out there, I can hardly get a coherent thought to penetrate my brainpan, but here…" He shrugged, his shoulder shifting against the mantel. "In here, everything seems to make sense. Maybe it's you."

"You always have me," Jacobi pointed out, "no matter where you are."

"Yes, but you're different in here, aren't you?"

"Am I?"

"Not too different," Alphonse assured him. "At least, no different than I am when I'm here."

"And how are you different?" Jacobi asked, his tone fond and amused.

He looked more open than usual, his expression softer, his eyes warmer, and the firelight flickered over his skin like gold. He looked so infinitely touchable that Alphonse couldn't help himself; he reached out to sweep his thumb over the line of Jacobi's jaw, and Jacobi waited patiently, his mouth curved in a soft smile.

"Braver, I hope," Alphonse said.

Steeling himself, he pushed off from the mantel and entered Jacobi's space, mirroring their earlier position in the bathroom. With one hand on Jacobi's forearm and the other around the back of his neck, he leaned up on his tiptoes and captured Jacobi's mouth in a kiss. Jacobi responded immediately, his eyes falling shut and his lips parting, kissing him back with one hand bracing Alphonse's elbow just as he had done before. He felt like comfort and familiarity and home and the warmest, simplest kind of love, like stepping into summer sunshine.

Alphonse's heart was so full it could burst. Breaking the kiss, his fingers still tangled in the hair at the back of Jacobi's head, he shut his eyes and exhaled in a long sigh, their noses touching.

"I've been missing out on an awful lot, haven't I?"

"That's easily resolved," Jacobi murmured.

Alphonse kissed him again, and the last of his nervousness melted away in the warm press of Jacobi's lips on his. His skin tingled everywhere Jacobi touched him, even through his clothes: one of Jacobi's hands at his elbow and the other at his waist, over his jacket. Alphonse's hands on Jacobi's chest and at the nape of his neck. He was hot all over, though the kiss itself was chaste, a mere pressing of mouth-to-mouth without any of the wetness that came from something deeper. But, chaste as it was, it was everything Alphonse wanted: sweet and steady and so full of love he could taste it.

When he pulled away, he felt light enough to spring up into the air and walk through the clouds, absolutely giddy with his success.

"Well," he said, giving Jacobi a pleased pat on the chest, "that wasn't so hard after all. I can't believe it took me so long to work up the nerve to do it."

"I never meant to make it difficult for you," Jacobi said, his hand migrating from Alphonse's elbow to rest on his shoulder, keeping him close. "I just needed to be sure you were committed to the course."

"I am! I was just so worried about scaring you off. Or, rather, not scaring, but offending, or some such thing. Anyway." Beaming, Alphonse took a step back to hold Jacobi at arm's length so he could see the whole of him at once. "I'd call that a ripping good test run, wouldn't you?"

Jacobi stilled, his posture turning statuesque. "A test run."

"Yes! A spot of practice before I build up to the real thing, what? It really is most convenient to have you here, you know. Not that I'd ever have tried anything like this before, of course. I wouldn't— Well, I wouldn't dream of it, as the saying goes. But now that the real Jacobi has made his intentions clear—I mean, the Jacobi out there in the waking world—well, it doesn't feel like such an overstepping of bounds to kiss you, even if you are only a figment of my imagination. You're still a figment wearing his face, and it would be awfully disrespectful to kiss you without his permission, whether you're real or not. If that makes sense. Am I making sense?"

"Sir," said Jacobi in an absolutely unreadable tone. "Do you know where you are?"

"I expect I'm asleep in bed. I've been having these dreams for ages, now. The two of us, here, like this, cosy as anything. But we've never kissed." Alphonse paused, an awful thought occurring to him. "Should I not have done that? Are dream characters their own people, and not just night-time imaginings swimming around the old soup of the subconscious?"

Alphonse had never seen Jacobi lost for words before.

"Er. Is it one of those things I'm not supposed to mention? I'm dreadfully sorry, old chap. I must have got the etiquette wrong. I didn't mean to imply that you weren't real. Most nights I just dream of the usual nonsense, you know: being run down in a fox hunt, or re-taking the old university exams, or some such. Turning up late to my own wedding. Nothing like this. Most dreams don't give me the opportunity to dwell on the mechanics of the thing, what? That's all philosophy, and you know how I'm rubbish at all that intellectual stuff. I really don't know what I'm doing here."

The longer Jacobi stared at him, the worse Alphonse felt. The cottage wasn't cosy anymore, but speared through with a terrible chill that cut him to the bone. But not the sort of chill brought on by poor weather: no, this was the sort that came from making an irreparable mistake, and being left to wallow in its consequences.

"Jacobi?" Alphonse ventured, at a terrible loss and unsure how to right whatever wrong he had committed.

"Perhaps you'd best return to your regular dreams for the night, sir," Jacobi said, still looking at him as if from the other side of some impassable void.

Everything went shimmery and translucent, the sturdy wooden walls and flashing fire giving way to the night sky, and Alphonse lifted up through the roof like a speck of pollen caught on the breeze. Weightless, he drifted through the atmosphere where the clouds cradled him like cotton batting, and brushed across his eyelids and tangled around his limbs, lulling him away to a deeper sleep.

Alphonse didn't know how long he drifted there, with flashes of other dreams darting behind his eyelids, snippets of other lives he could be leading that never coalesced into anything solid. He pulled away from each one that approached him, bent on returning to the cottage and finding Jacobi again, but the clouds wrapped themselves ever tighter around his body until his head was all muddled with the heaviness of sleep, and he gave up and lost himself to oblivion for a time.

♦ ♦ ♦

He woke at three in the a.m., a mere two hours after going to bed. Sitting bolt upright with a gasp, he rubbed the sleep from his eyes and, ignoring the protests from his body urging him to stay in bed a while longer, he swung his feet to the floor and groped for his slippers and dressing gown.

"Idiot," he groaned, tying the sash and running his hands through his hair.

THE BACHELOR'S VALET

He had gone to bed with it still wet, and it had dried in wild waves that would take ages to tame. He didn't care. The only thing that mattered was Jacobi. Jacobi, who had bathed him and touched him and kissed him back, because he was as real in that cottage as he was in Alphonse's flat, and Alphonse was a colossal twit for not realising it from the start. Of course the cottage dream was a comfortable respite from his normal subconscious dalliances: because it wasn't a proper dream at all.

And he had gone and muddled everything up again, as he always did. His first instinct was to take the whole mess to Aaliyah as he had done before and hope that she could fix it, but he was tired of letting other people deal with his mistakes. He wanted to lay things out plainly for Jacobi with no more nervousness or second-guessing getting in the way.

So determined, he propelled himself from his bed and strode to the bedroom door, turning down the hallway and heading straight for Jacobi's quarters.

Jacobi's door was shut, as it always was at night, and Alphonse pulled up short before it, one hand frozen where it was raised to knock. A crumb of doubt entered his mind. If Jacobi was still asleep and Alphonse really had been immersed in an especially befuddling dream designed to trick him—

Then Jacobi would forgive him, surely. Better to risk an interrupted night's sleep than to risk letting this go unresolved.

Alphonse knocked on the door, two soft raps that might allow a heavier sleeper to ignore them (which

Jacobi was not and had never been), before turning the handle and easing himself through the crack in the doorway.

Jacobi was awake, and, Alphonse was relieved to see, apparently had been prior to his knocking. He was sitting on the edge of his mattress with his feet on the floor and his elbows resting on his knees, hands clasped, looking the least polished Alphonse had ever seen him. But then, Alphonse had never seen him at night before. Not like this. Not barefoot and in his pyjamas, the bedcovers folded back and sheets rumpled in evidence of where he had lain, his hair not yet fixed in place with pomade but curling gently over his forehead, a single perfect strand escaping the rest to bob over one eye. He looked tired in a way Alphonse had never seen before, and not just because it was the middle of the night. A pair of glasses rested on his bedside table, thin wire frames glinting in the dim lamplight.

"That was you," Alphonse said. "It's always been you, hasn't it?"

"Yes. It was always me."

"But how?" Alphonse asked helplessly. "How did you set up shop in my dreams like that?"

"I didn't. You came into mine."

Alphonse stared at him, stunned. "But I don't know how to do that."

"No, sir."

Jacobi rose to his feet, straightening his pyjama top and running his fingers through his hair, disrupting the curl and smoothing it back from his forehead. Despite his night-time attire, the transformation was immediate, and some of the gnawing anxiety in Alphonse's chest eased at the sight. Jacobi was still himself, still his immaculate valet, capable of solving or explaining anything.

"I'll put the kettle on, sir, and then we should have a talk about dreamwalking."

Alphonse trailed Jacobi to the kitchen, crowding close to his heels but resisting the urge to reach out and touch, unsure of his welcome after that debacle of a dream. Evidence of their earlier dinner was still strewn about, dirty dishes piled in the sink and red-stained wineglasses lined up along the counter. Jacobi prepared two mugs of chamomile in silence, handing one to Alphonse before guiding him to the living room and quietly gesturing for Alphonse to take a seat. Alphonse sank into his chair, mug cradled between both hands and knees pressed tightly together to keep from trembling.

"I realised what had happened straight away, the first time you wandered into my dreams," Jacobi said, still standing, and gazing into his own tea like it was easier to address his words to the steam. "I didn't mention it then because you seemed altogether oblivious, and when we spoke the next morning, you didn't indicate any memory of it. I put it down to a harmless accident, and didn't pursue the matter. Which was, of course, in hindsight a mistake."

"I don't remember the first time I dreamt of you in that cottage," Alphonse confessed, fiddling with the handle of his mug. "It always seemed so familiar, right from the very beginning."

"I don't think you were fully lucid the first few times you visited. Which was to be expected, if you weren't dreamwalking intentionally, and had never done it before. So, by the time you achieved lucidity, your subconscious was already familiar with the setting."

"I *wasn't* doing it intentionally, and I *hadn't* done it before! At least, I don't think I've ever done it before. Maybe I've wandered into all sorts of people's dreams without ever noticing." Alphonse anxiously sought out Jacobi's gaze. "Is that possible? Have I been intruding on other people's sleep for years without realising it?"

"It's highly unlikely, sir," Jacobi reassured him. "Unintentional dreamwalking generally occurs only between people who share a close understanding of one another's minds in the waking world. It would be very difficult for you to slip into a stranger's dreams without a great deal of practice beforehand."

Alphonse sank back into his chair. "Well, that's a relief. Though it doesn't make me feel any better about intruding on yours."

Jacobi retreated, eyes averted once more as he paced to the mantelpiece and set his cup of tea down upon it. "You weren't responsible for your actions, sir. I should have immediately taken it upon myself to explain the matter to you, especially when you appeared for a second time. By the time you had established a pattern and were undeniably lucid, I had no excuse. But I'm ashamed to say that by then, I had grown attached to your company in my dreams, and was reluctant to sever that bond. It was selfish, and it did neither of us any favours."

"So you just let me wander into your head whenever I wanted, all willy-nilly?" Alphonse asked incredulously.

"Yes, sir." Jacobi turned to look at him for the first time since retreating, his expression one of weariness and regret. "Because you see, my second mistake was in believing that with your newfound lucidity came an understanding of your actions. I thought you knew what you were doing, sir, and that we had an unspoken agreement not to discuss it."

"But *how?*" Alphonse asked for the second time. "You know I haven't got any magic!"

"Obviously, sir, you do."

Alphonse upset his tea all over his lap and jumped out of his chair with a yelped curse. The liquid wasn't hot enough to scald, but it was still mightily uncomfortable. By the time Jacobi reached his side, he was frantically patting himself down as if that would help. Putting one hand on Alphonse's shoulder to still him, Jacobi drew a quick sign in the air and made a swiping motion with his other hand, and immediately, Alphonse's pyjamas were dry again as if nothing had happened.

"You have magic out here, too!" Alphonse's mind was running in circles with all these revelations. "You know, I always suspected you did."

"Yes, sir. I've always felt it in better taste to practice discreetly."

"And *I* have magic."

Jacobi knowing spellwork wasn't any shock at all, not with how he was so talented in every other aspect of his life, and especially not after seeing him perform magic so casually in their shared dreams. But Alphonse couldn't wrap his head around having magic himself. It went against absolutely everything he knew about his person. He had never had magic, not a single drop of the stuff. He couldn't even understand the fundamentals of magical theory, never mind how to orchestrate a spell. It was incomprehensible that he should have the kind of power to go strolling through other people's heads without noticing it.

"I can explain the mechanics of dreamwalking, but I'm afraid I can't explain anything about your latent powers," Jacobi said regretfully. "I'm simply not trained in such matters."

Alphonse dropped back into his chair like his strings had been cut. "Don't bother about the mechanics of anything," he said, flapping one hand. "I won't understand a lick of it anyway. I just need to know the basics to make sure I don't do it again."

Jacobi made a neutral sound. "I can help you with that if you wish it, sir."

Alphonse took a closer look at him. "Or," he hazarded, "if you like having me around your little cottage, maybe you could teach me how to visit on purpose."

An imperceptible line of tension in Jacobi's shoulders eased. "I could do that."

"Because," Alphonse continued, "I've grown awfully fond of the place, what? It's the funniest thing. It was there that I realised I was attracted to you in the first place, you see. And it was only in the wake of one of those dreams, trying to explain to Aaliyah how they made me feel, that I realised I was altogether in love with you."

Jacobi finally looked at him, dark lashes framing wide eyes.

"I was a complete idiot about it, of course, not being able to come out and say it properly, but it was so unforgivably inappropriate, what? With you being my valet and all. The timing was a complete mess from top to bottom, and then I went and made it worse at every turn." Sucking in a deep breath like the air was courage itself, Alphonse shed his insecurities and stood, crossing the room to take both of Jacobi's hands in his. "I'm saying it now, right to your face, when I'm not drunk or drugged or dreaming, so you'll know that I mean it. I love you, Jacobi, and probably have done from the day I met you. It's just that my brain takes so long to catch up to my feelings. You know I'm hopeless at puzzling things out."

"I know, sir," Jacobi said softly.

"I just wish you had told me that I was in love with you sooner. It could have saved us all this trouble."

"I could have, sir," Jacobi agreed. "It just seemed like something you should arrive at in your own time."

"I suppose so. Although, to be clear, I didn't. Aaliyah pushed me into it, and thank god, I say. If I'd been left to figure it out on my own it might have taken me another five years."

Jacobi hummed, lowering his eyes as if to hide the smile curved on his lips. "I might have prompted you to address the matter sooner than that."

"I should hope so." Alphonse worried his lip for a second. "Look, old thing, I hate to presume on matters of the heart—or any other matters, really—but do you… That is, do you feel…"

"Yes, sir."

"Yes?"

"I do love you. I have loved you for quite some time."

Alphonse could scarcely contain the champagne fizz of emotion that bubbled up from his chest. Pressing both hands over his mouth to keep from whooping, he asked hopefully through his fingers, "Does this mean you'll drop the *sirs* and call me by my name now? Like you do in the dreams?"

"If you like. But I must insist on keeping such things formal in public."

"Yes, of course. It wouldn't do to tarnish your reputation."

"Or yours," Jacobi pointed out.

"Pfft. Privately, though—"

"Alphonse."

Alphonse froze. He had heard his name on Jacobi's lips before, but it hit differently, knowing it was real. The sound made him warm all over, the champagne bubbles turning to a whole flock of butterflies in his stomach, flapping up a whirlwind of delight.

Before Alphonse had time to recover, Jacobi stepped forward, caught Alphonse's hands to lower them from his face, and kissed him. His hands rested atop Alphonse's shoulders and their mouths slotted perfectly together, and Alphonse's brain spluttered to a stop. Jacobi was a far cry from Alphonse's youthful fumbles. Elegant and self-assured, his kiss was a warm front of pressure with no roving tongues or groping hands to distract from the simple act. When he parted his lips minutely, gently coaxing Alphonse to follow suit, the sensation came as a burst of heat, full of promise. Jacobi pulled back before it was fulfilled, and Alphonse was instantly bereft. He chased the kiss, needily pressing himself against Jacobi's front and leaning up to steal another taste of him.

"We shouldn't," Jacobi murmured, his lips grazing Alphonse's forehead. "You're still drunk from dinner."

"Oh, hardly! Come to bed with me."

Jacobi stilled, and Alphonse took the opportunity to attach himself more firmly to the man, clamping on like a lamprey eel and hiding his face in Jacobi's throat. Now that they had finally said everything out loud, he never wanted to let go again.

"I'm not drunk," Alphonse said, nibbling at Jacobi's jaw. "Tipsy, yes, but not drunk."

"You only realised you wanted this a day ago. I think you can wait a little longer."

"I'll wait as long as I have to, but come to bed with me anyway. Just to sleep," Alphonse begged. "If I'm going to come stumbling into your dreams again, we might as well be in the same room when it happens. It's not like we can get more intimate than dream-sharing, what?"

"If dream-sharing is the most intimate activity you can imagine," Jacobi said in a low voice that sent thrills through Alphonse's core, "then clearly I must broaden your horizons."

CHAPTER TWELVE

AN OLD-FASHIONED EXCHANGING OF RINGS AND VOWS

They lay side by side in Jacobi's bed, facing each other as they shared a single pillow, knees touching under the covers. Alphonse had one arm under the pillow and the other closing the short distance between them to tangle with Jacobi's fingers. He explored Jacobi's hands one at a time, quietly marvelling at the strength and dexterity in their form. The callouses on his fingertips, the neatness of his nails, and the subtle whorls of his fingerprints. And the scar from the iron at the base of Jacobi's thumb. Alphonse traced it from top to bottom, lip held between his teeth in concentration. Up close, the scar was smaller than he had thought, just a tiny mark, really, and smooth to the touch. Otherwise, it felt no different from the rest of his skin, which helped mitigate some of Alphonse's guilt over causing it.

"It doesn't hurt?" he murmured.

"It barely hurt at the time," Jacobi replied.

To Alphonse's disappointment, holding hands and touching knees was the extent of their physical contact, despite Jacobi's talk of broadening horizons. Though he couldn't be too disappointed, what with the two of them under the covers together, so much like his earlier bath-time fantasy.

"Tell me more about the cottage?" Alphonse requested. "It is a real place? Whenever I dream about real places they always get so tangled up in my head, sprawling out with extra rooms or set in some strange location that doesn't map onto the real world. But I suppose it must be different if you've got that kind of control over your dreams."

"I made it up, actually," Jacobi replied. "I might have known a place somewhat like it when I was a child, but I designed that precise cottage as my own private sanctuary. It has no real-world counterpart."

"You mean to tell me you're an architect on top of everything else? Your talents truly know no bounds."

"I wouldn't want to test my architectural skills outside of a dream, but thank you."

"Can you teach me how to do that? Build places, and whatnot?"

"If you like. You will need some degree of patience in the beginning, though. It's a matter of focus and imagination rather than spellwork, but it's still a muscle that will need to be strengthened before you find yourself proficient with it."

"Well, as long as I've got you for a teacher, I don't think I'll go too far astray." Alphonse paused. "What about the cat? Did you make her up, too?"

"No, I don't know where she comes from. Cats will do as they please, after all. I call her Tabitha."

Alphonse took a moment to ponder the concept of dreamwalking cats. It must mean that cats had their own kind of magic, which he didn't find as surprising as he should have. If any animal were inclined to magic, he would have thought cats to be the most likely, after all.

"But I don't think we're going to be exploring any dream architecture tonight," Jacobi said, cutting into Alphonse's line of thought. "It's almost four in the morning, and we should both get some sleep. Some real sleep, that is. Dreamsharing is all well and good, but lucidity doesn't lend itself to proper rest, I'm afraid."

"I don't want to sleep," Alphonse confessed, running his thumb over Jacobi's knuckles. "I want to stay like this forever, talking to you like tomorrow's never going to come. All tucked up and cosy under the blankets where nothing can interrupt us. What's sleep good for, anyway?"

"A romantic thought, but tomorrow will always come, and you're going to feel worse for it if you try to stay awake for twenty-four hours straight."

"But Jacobi, I'm in love!" Alphonse wriggled closer until their noses touched and he could steal a kiss between every breath he took. "I'm much too in love to ever sleep again, I think."

"Would you like me to help with that?"

"With one of those herbal remedies you've got stashed away in the kitchen?"

"I don't have any herbal sleeping remedies," Jacobi said, turning slightly sheepish for the first time in the five years Alphonse had known him.

"What? Of course you have. What else have you been putting in my tea all this time?"

Lifting the hand that hadn't been claimed by Alphonse's amorous attentions, Jacobi conjured a tiny drop of magic that sat like a pebble of fresh dew on the pad of his index finger. It was amber, the colour of sunlight shining through fresh honey, and it carried the sharp sent of citrus, strong enough to set Alphonse's mouth to watering.

"I say, I know that smell. Have you been using magic on me all this time, without my knowing?"

"I'm afraid so, though I hasten to add, never without your permission."

"What other magic have you been doing? Do you get my clothes to iron themselves when I'm not around?"

"Certainly not." Jacobi's tone was affronted. "I assure you, every skill on which I pride myself as a valet is one hundred percent earned through non-magical means. Unfortunately, there are no herbal sleeping aids that work as effectively as the pharmaceutical ones, and this particular magical concoction has no side effects or complications in comparison to the chemical drugs.

And I dislike offering a second-rate choice when a better option is within easy reach."

"Fair enough," Alphonse allowed. "I can't argue with your logic."

Jacobi lifted his finger infinitesimally. "Then, may I?"

Alphonse burrowed deeper into his pillow, snuggling up as close to Jacobi as he could get. Their legs were firmly tangled and their joined hands pressed up against Jacobi's chest so Alphonse could feel his heart thumping steadily through his pyjamas. "Go on, then."

Jacobi pressed the drop of magic against Alphonse's forehead, right in between his eyes. His fingertip was a warm pressure against the skin as the magic melted straight into Alphonse's brain. The smell of summer oranges hung in the air for a moment before dissolving like gentle perfume into Alphonse's mussed waves. Alphonse shut his eyes, letting the magic wash over and through him, and fell asleep with his head tucked against Jacobi's shoulder as the man dropped a kiss and a soft good night into his hair.

♦ ♦ ♦

The next week passed in a dizzying rush of stolen touches and clandestine kisses. They fell into one another as often as possible: morning kisses over breakfast with Jacobi's fingers carding through Alphonse's hair, and pressed up against the door after returning from some outing, or traded lazily after dinner and a glass of wine. But, to Alphonse's dismay, they hadn't shared either a bed or a dream again since the night of the dinner party. There had been no broadening of horizons, and Alphonse was beginning to suspect that Jacobi rather enjoyed drawing the matter out and pushing Alphonse to the limits of his patience.

Finally, after seven torturous days of Jacobi insisting that they part ways every night when bedtime rolled around, he appeared in Alphonse's doorway just as Alphonse was slipping his tie from his collar.

"I have something for you," Jacobi said.

It was a perfectly innocent statement on its own, and had in the past heralded anything from bills to invitations to midnight snacks. But in the past week it had taken on new meaning, shimmering with possibilities that had Alphonse positively squirming at the potential.

"Oh?" he asked, trying not to sound too curious.

Reaching into his inner breast pocket, Jacobi withdrew a small, square box and held it out in the palm of his hand. Tossing his tie onto the bed, Alphonse reached out hesitantly, suddenly trembling with anticipation. The box was black velvet, soft and solid to the touch.

"Is this…?"

"Miss Bailey's selection for Miss Kaddour."

Alphonse plucked the box up and pried open the lid. In a bed of cream-coloured satin sat nestled a delicate ring topped with a diamond cut in the shape of a little cluster of jasmine blossoms, their star-like petals spiralling out in geometric perfection. It flashed even in the dim light of the bedroom, sparkling as he turned the box this way and that.

"It's beautiful."

"Miss Bailey assures me it is perfectly to Miss Kaddour's taste."

"And we're to pretend that I chose it myself?"

"In company, yes."

He nodded, entranced. It was a stunning piece of craftmanship, and if it meant something between Jasmine and Aaliyah, then all the better. He cleared his throat and snapped the box shut again. "Very good. Excellent. Well done indeed."

"There was something else."

"What, not the wedding rings, too?" Alphonse joked.

Wordlessly, Jacobi handed him a second box, the exact size and shape as the first, and something caught in Alphonse's throat. He cracked the lid with shaking fingers, and there sat a second ring: much simpler than the first, but eye-catching nonetheless, with an understated silver band and a single, tiny diamond set in the crown.

"And what's this?" Alphonse asked, his voice trembling.

"I chose it for you. If I may?"

Jacobi tugged the ring from its nest, waiting for Alphonse to offer up his hand. Alphonse held his breath as Jacobi slid the ring onto his finger, over the knuckle, for it to sit perfectly snug at the base. Once the ring was in place, Jacobi continued to hold his hand, his skin warm and dry against Alphonse's palm. For his part, Alphonse had broken into a mild sweat. The ring's band was lustrous and shiny, the diamond glittering. An engagement ring.

"It suits you," Jacobi said, sounding pleased as he stroked his thumb over Alphonse's knuckles. "If you wish to wear it—"

"I do," Alphonse said hoarsely.

"Say it was from Miss Kaddour, as she'll say hers was from you. It may not be traditional for men to wear engagement rings as women do, but I don't believe anyone will question it."

Alphonse fell quiet for a minute. "When I asked you back at the start of all this, you said that you didn't see marriage as being in the books for you."

"I did say that."

"On account of your only love at the time being unrequited." He dropped his gaze. "And not being able to devote the proper time to a spouse outside of work, and all that."

"I don't think it's possible for me to spend *more* time with you," Jacobi said, amused, "so I'm not worried on that count."

"No, we were practically married already, weren't we? Living together for the past five years and all. Funny how things turn out. I never wanted marriage for myself, but this is good, isn't it? This will be good."

"We'll make it good," Jacobi promised. "Although, it must be noted that my first and only love wasn't as unrequited as I had thought, which I find very gratifying."

Alphonse startled. "Wait, what? Who's that, then?"

Jacobi looked at him steadily, their hands still clasped between them, until Alphonse figured it out.

"Oh! Really? Why, I had no idea!"

"I know," Jacobi said placidly. "You weren't meant to."

Alphonse sniffed to hide his warm glow. "Well. I suppose I can't blame you for not saying anything. Not with how I handled things on my end of the equation."

"We got everything figured out in the end. That's what's important."

That was what Aaliyah had told him, wasn't it? If things weren't alright, then it wasn't the end yet. He would have been annoyed with her being right yet again if Jacobi's words weren't nudging him up against a waterfall of tears.

His throat too gummed up with emotion to speak, Alphonse barely managed to eke out, "I don't have a ring for you, though."

"Seeing you wear this is enough," Jacobi said simply. "This, and the wedding ring. Though I thought that after the ceremony I might add an inscription to their inner bands, if that is amenable."

"Whatever you like." Alphonse withdrew his hand in order to run his thumb along the ring, rotating it around his finger. The metal was cool and sleek and wonderfully grounding. "Is this how people feel at the altar, do you think? Funny how something so small can feel so permanent."

"It's as permanent as you want it to be, whether you wish to wear it or not."

"I'll wear it," Alphonse swore immediately, "and I do want it to be permanent. I want you here with me forever, Jacobi, do you understand? Come hell or high water or marriages or whatever else life cares to throw at us. And I'll buy you a ring, too. Don't worry," he added, noting Jacobi's imperceptible flinch. "I'll drag Aaliyah along to make sure I don't choose anything too egregious." Stepping close, he flung both arms around Jacobi's neck and said into his throat, "I want you to feel just as I'm feeling in this moment."

"And how is that?" Jacobi asked, as if Alphonse weren't leaking his feelings all over the place.

"Like I belong with someone. I've known I've belonged with you from the first day I met you. It feels so indescribably right to be by your side. And having a ring doesn't change that, but I want you to feel like you belong with me just as much."

"I do. Very much so."

Alphonse drew back just far enough to look Jacobi in the eye. "Hold up, now. Did we just exchange vows?"

"It does appear that way."

"Well, that wasn't nearly so stressful as I imagined it going at the altar. I suppose if I'd had more time to prepare I would have worked myself up into an awful state of nerves, especially at the thought of all those people watching me blunder my way through it. I must say, I much prefer the idea of making promises in private like this."

"As a matter of fact," Jacobi said quietly, his hands at Alphonse's waist as if they were about to share the most intimate of slow dances, "this is how people used to be married. Before the necessity of the church being involved, or requiring an ordained minister, two people would exchange vows in private much like this. And that union would be considered just as legitimate as any marriage that took place before a priest and a hundred witnesses."

Alphonse shivered and pressed himself closer along Jacobi's front. "Is that so?" A thought occurred to him and he broke into a smile, tipping his face up to look at Jacobi. "Then that would make this our wedding night, what?"

"It would," Jacobi confirmed, his eyelashes sweeping his cheeks as his mouth curled up and he held Alphonse tighter, like there was absolutely nowhere else in the world he would rather be.

"Are you going to go on keeping me waiting before you take me to bed? Or is this, with the rings and all—"

Jacobi cut him off with a kiss and Alphonse melted. "No," Jacobi said against his mouth, "I won't make you wait anymore."

Alphonse pulled Jacobi forward by his lapels, walking himself backwards until he hit the edge of his bed. There, he stopped, and turned his attention to divesting Jacobi of his outer layers as quickly as possible. The challenge in such an act was to do it without breaking their kiss, but it was a challenge Alphonse was all too eager to meet. For once in his life, Jacobi seemed unconcerned about the state of either of their clothes, for which Alphonse was appreciative. If the man had insisted they stop to hang their jackets up,

Alphonse might have combusted from sheer frustration.

But Jacobi insisted on no such thing, being wholly occupied with stripping Alphonse's shirt from his shoulders and then turning his attention to all that bare skin. Alphonse delighted in every touch, relishing the way Jacobi's fingertips skimmed his shoulder blades before dragging down firmly over his ribs, the hot press of his mouth against his collarbones, the caress of his breath against his throat. And as Jacobi explored Alphonse's body, Alphonse wasted no time in uncovering Jacobi's. Valet uniform cast aside, Alphonse swung himself onto the bed and drew Jacobi down with him, every inch of his attention fixed on the man's body. He had never seen it before, and he wanted to memorise every inch of it. The moles scattered like constellations over Jacobi's shoulders, the trail of black hair that drew a line down from his bellybutton to disappear under his trousers.

Their trousers were the next thing to be shed. Alphonse kicked his off and flung them to the floor without trying to make the act seductive. He was far more occupied with unbuttoning Jacobi's and pulling them past his hips, too impatient to wait for Jacobi's cooperation. It was a disorganised affair all around, with Alphonse laughing at his own ineptitude in between kisses, and Jacobi trying to direct him to more efficient means without much success. But finally, they were free of their clothes. Alphonse knelt in the centre of the bed clad only in his underthings while Jacobi sat on the side of the mattress, his feet on the floor and his torso turned to face Alphonse.

"Tell me what you want," Jacobi said.

Alphonse wanted a hundred million different things: kisses and touches and acts he didn't even know the names of, every single thing that could be shared between two people. Some of those things, he had done before, but as he stared at Jacobi—his dark-eyed, perfect man whom he had never seen simmering like this, like he had some unquenchable heat burning just under his skin— As he stared, every single one of those past experiences fled his brain and left him a blank slate. Whatever they did together, it would be as if it were Alphonse's first time.

"I want you," Alphonse said.

Jacobi leaned in for another kiss, one hand coming to the back of Alphonse's neck, the other at his chest as he bore him back against the pillows. Alphonse went easily, pulling Jacobi down on top of him, thrilled at the feeling of being pinned.

"You have me," Jacobi told him. "In whatever way you want."

"You can't expect me to come up with specifics right now," Alphonse said breathlessly. "You were the one talking about the expanding of boundaries, and whatnot. And we both know you're the one who's better off in charge."

"Very well, then. I'll be in charge."

Alphonse surrendered to the pillows and the surety of Jacobi's hands, a grin splitting his face as he hooked one leg around the back of Jacobi's thigh, drawing him closer. Jacobi went with a smile. Not one of those secretive little smiles that could only be seen if one were really paying attention, but a smile that touched his whole face, even if it was still subtler than Alphonse's full-watt beam.

"Let's start with something simple and work our way up," Jacobi suggested, slipping one clever hand under the waistband of Alphonse's drawers, and Alphonse certainly had no objection to that.

♦ ♦ ♦

It was late morning and overcast with terrifically dark November clouds, but the impending rain wasn't enough to dampen Alphonse's mood. The wedding was in seven months to the day, and everything felt like it was falling into place. For once, Alphonse wasn't being buffeted by the currents of such happenings, but floating along contentedly in their wake.

Aaliyah elbowed him in the side. "You're looking pleased with yourself."

Alphonse gave her a sunny smile and offered her his arm. "Am I?"

"You dog." She linked their arms together, and side by side they marched up to the front door of the Hollyhock estate. "You got with Jacobi, didn't you?"

"I might have. Hardly polite conversation though, is it?"

She leaned into him, bearing down until he staggered, losing his balance with a laugh. "That depends entirely on how far you took things. Did you kiss him?"

"I'm not going to tell you!"

"You're blushing! I bet you did. What else did you do? Was there any…?" Bobbing her eyebrows, she made a crude gesture with one hand, and Alphonse burst out in shocked laughter as he pushed through the doors.

"Aaliyah! You can't ask me that! My mother could be just around the corner!"

"That's why I didn't say it out loud."

"You absolute devil." Tucking himself back against her side, they made it a few yards down the corridor before he added under his breath, "And yes, if you must know, we did do something along those lines, and I hope we do it again, and more."

"Ha! So, was I right? About how it was entirely safe to share your feelings with Jacobi, and that everything would work out alright once you did?"

"Isn't it too soon to say that everything has worked out?" Alphonse wondered aloud. "There's still our wedding to get through, not to mention this very luncheon. I won't consider myself out of the woods until I've escaped my mother's thorny grasp, at the very least."

"So dramatic," Aaliyah teased. "She only wants to talk about the guest list and the flower arrangements."

Alphonse shuddered. "Yes, I'll leave all that to you two, if you don't mind. If I sit very still, maybe she won't notice me. Just give me a nudge when I'm expected to chime in and make a sound of agreement, please."

"Yes, dear," Aaliyah said dryly.

Alphonse's mother greeted them at the door to the conservatory, offering Aaliyah a smile and a compliment before turning her scrutinising regard to her unfortunate son. Alphonse gave her a weak smile in return and a kiss on the cheek, holding Aaliyah's hand like she was his lifeline as they took their seats amid the jungle of greenery. The plants seemed to have doubled in size and quantity both since his last visit.

"You're both looking well," Mrs. Hollyhock said as the maid brought in a platter of sandwiches and fresh tea, setting it on the table between them. "The engagement is going smoothly, I hope?" She eyed Alphonse. "No hiccups?"

"Everything is just splendid, Mrs. Hollyhock," Aaliyah said brightly, giving Alphonse a supportive pat on the knee. "I couldn't ask for more in fiancé."

Though her disbelief was plain to see, Mrs. Hollyhock thawed. "I must say, that does my heart good to hear, Miss Kaddour. You know how I had despaired of finding a suitable match for my Alphonse, but now I can almost confidently say that you are everything I could have hoped for him."

"Almost confidently?" Alphonse asked.

Mrs. Hollyhock took a delicate sip of tea, narrowing her eyes at him over the rim of her cup. "Let's get you both through the wedding first, and then I will re-evaluate."

Aaliyah laughed, the sound like tinkling bells, and Alphonse had to hide his own laugh in response behind one hand, knowing that her real mirth sounded far more like the barking of wild dogs. He preferred her genuine laugh, though he could appreciate that his mother likely wouldn't.

"Shall we save the intricate details of wedding planning until after we've eaten?" Aaliyah suggested, for once seeming to take pity on her poor companion.

"Yes, let's," Mrs. Hollyhock allowed, to Alphonse's great relief.

They passed the luncheon in idle chitchat, nibbling their way through the little sandwiches and then a plate of biscuits, and for the first time in a long time in his mother's presence, Alphonse felt that perhaps everything really would be alright. Even after the talk turned to wedding planning, it wasn't enough to burst the bright, happy bubble that had taken up residence in his chest, and he found it easy to agree with whatever comments his mother threw his way. Aaliyah did her best to deflect most of Mrs. Hollyhock's attention from Alphonse, but even the bits that shot through her defences, Alphonse didn't find as stinging as he normally might. In fact, the lunch passed in an absolute breeze, and at the end of it, though he was by no means sad to take his leave from the conservatory, neither was he running full tilt for the door.

"You look happy," his mother said, catching him by the hands as they said their goodbyes. She said it in a funny sort of voice, peering into his eyes as if searching for some trick to be revealed. "The two of you together… As glad as I am that your union took, it's not something I would have expected."

"How do you mean?" Alphonse asked. "You set this whole thing up; surely you must have expected it to take?"

"Oh, I always expected you to make a perfectly fine pair. But this? You're practically glowing, dear. The both of you."

Alphonse looked at Aaliyah, who was of course much better at keeping her cool in the face of maternal scrutiny. She just smiled and linked her arm through Alphonse's, leaning against his side in the very picture of infatuation.

"I hardly expected it either," she said easily, wearing a blinding smile. "But it's true: we are very much in love, and we couldn't be happier."

And it was true. They just weren't in love with each other.

CHAPTER THIRTEEN

OR, THAT WHICH IS ALSO KNOWN AS AN EPILOGUE

It was less of a blow than Alphonse had expected, leaving his flat for a house. He still had all his things, after all, and Aaliyah was more than happy to let him keep his car, provided he let her have a go at it whenever she liked. And, most importantly, he still had Jacobi.

It was Jacobi who had arranged the buying of the house, in fact. He set it all up while Alphonse was swamped with wedding planning, appearing at Alphonse's elbow now and then to have him sign something before whisking off as quickly as he had appeared. It had all been so awfully hectic that the first time Alphonse saw the house was the mid-June day that he moved into it. They drove there straight after the wedding, all four of them piled into the car. Jacobi was behind the wheel with Jasmine beside him and Alphonse and Aaliyah side by side in the back seat to give their wedding guests one last view of the happy couple, white ribbons trailing from the back of the car like a school of airy fish.

The house was still in a fashionable part of London, albeit in a quieter neighbourhood, and when they pulled up in front of it, Alphonse couldn't bring himself to feel anything but giddy elation at the prospect of starting a new stage of his life. The house was a handsome thing done up in dark brick, nestled snuggly in between its neighbours, guarded by a swirling wrought iron gate decorated with little bird patterns throughout, and a magnificently tall tree resplendent in shimmering leaves.

Apparently, everyone was familiar with the house except for Alphonse, and Aaliyah traipsed through the rooms with great gaiety, pulling him along as she showed off all the house's features as if daring him to compare it to his old flat and find it wanting. But he couldn't keep the smile from his face. Not just on account of the house, which seemed a fine place to hang his hat, but on account of the whole day, and all the days leading up to it: all those kisses shared and promises made and vows exchanged.

"Do you like it?" Jacobi asked quietly, once the whirlwind tour was over and the girls were settled in one of their rooms for a moment of post-wedding privacy. "Aaliyah wants to paint all the walls in colours of her choosing. I encouraged her to discuss it with you first, but of course I expect her to do as she pleases."

Alphonse looked around the empty rooms, some of the walls blank and others still clinging to their old paper. "I think a spot of colour would be marvellous. She'll do it up brightly, I imagine. It'll be like living in Kew Gardens year-round. What do you think? It's as much your house as it is hers or mine, after all."

"I have no objection, though I might like something calmer for my own room. A sedate blue-grey, perhaps."

"I'm sure that can be arranged."

Alphonse found Jacobi's hand and twined their fingers together, just because he could. The ring Alphonse had bought him, a broad silver thing with darker bands round the outside, sat securely on Jacobi's finger like it had always been there. No one could see the cursive A + J etched on the band's underside, identical to the initials etched on Alphonse's own ring, but Alphonse saw the design behind his eyelids every time he blinked.

"Come and see the garden," Jacobi suggested.

Alphonse followed Jacobi to the back door, which opened to a small patio. Hydrangeas, with their puffs of pinks, purples, and blues, stood on either side of the door, nestled up close to the house, and the air was balmy with midsummer cheer, the hours long and meandering before sunset. The garden was enclosed by a tall stone wall with a cluster of trees at the far end, and flower beds hosting all manner of plants and bushes lined up on either side. They weren't cultivated in the manner of Kew, with every flower in its proper place, but rather in the haphazard style of a wild meadow, with all sorts of bright flowers growing up amid the long yellow wisps of grass like they had a mind of their own. Poppies and cornflowers and chamomile, buttercups and clover and blossoming nettles all bobbed in the evening gold like Alphonse wasn't in London at all, but somewhere quieter and infinitely more private. They could put chairs out on the patio, or perhaps further back under the shade of one of those trees. The image seemed like something from a dream.

"I knew a proper cottage would be far too rustic for your tastes," Jacobi said, his body a warm line against Alphonse's side. "But I thought you might enjoy having such a garden in the waking world." He pressed a kiss to Alphonse's temple. "As a reminder that you don't only have me in your dreams."

"I like that reminder."

Smiling, Jacobi leaned down to catch Alphonse in a proper kiss, and Alphonse stretched up to wrap both his arms around Jacobi's neck, pressing their chests together and revelling in the heat of it. The walls were far too high to spy over, and they had an entire house to themselves, Aaliyah and Jasmine notwithstanding. But they didn't count, not when they were in on it. Alphonse had never felt freer in his life.

Even if the walls had been lower, it wouldn't have mattered. If they couldn't kiss in the garden, they could always kiss in their dreams. Alphonse's control of his dreamwalking had blossomed in the past few months under Jacobi's tutelage—not to the point of expertise, but enough that Alphonse could choose when and how to enter Jacobi's dreams. How his magic had gone unnoticed for so long, he still had no idea, and perhaps he never would. It didn't particularly concern him. Flashy party tricks to show off to his peers were nothing compared to the private thrill of dreamwalking with Jacobi, after all.

When he pulled back from the kiss to catch his breath, still pressed against Jacobi's front like he never wanted them to part, the garden was lit up with little orbs of glowing light, bobbing around like lazily contented fireflies. They washed everything in soft yellow, and when Alphonse held out a hand, one floated over to kiss his fingertip, leaving his skin tingling with the tiniest brush of electricity.

"I want this all the time," Alphonse said, keeping his voice quiet like if he spoke too loudly, he might bring reality crashing down around them. All he wanted to do was bask in the garden of his brand-new house where everything was safe and warm and friendly, and stay tucked up in Jacobi's embrace forever.

"You can have it," Jacobi said, like it was that simple.

Well, Alphonse thought, *why shouldn't it be?*

The largest of the orbs floated over to the stone wall, and Alphonse followed it, Jacobi a step behind him, their fingers still tangled together. The ball of light hovered as if waiting for them to catch up, slowly dipping up and down, illuminating one of the bushes that nudged up against the stone. The leaves shivered and Alphonse took a startled step back, colliding with Jacobi, who steadied him and then knelt down with one hand extended. From under the bush stepped a brown and grey tabby cat with pale green eyes, walking straight up to him like she had been waiting, and pushed her face against his hand.

"Hello, Tabitha," Jacobi murmured, running his hand down her back.

When she had greeted him, she continued on to Alphonse, who stood stock still in wonderment as she twined around his ankles, her tail raised high as she pressed her full weight against his shins. Jacobi scooped the cat up to nestle in the crook of his elbow before returning to Alphonse's side, touching his other hand to the small of Alphonse's back. Alphonse slung one arm around Jacobi's waist and leaned in to rest his head against his shoulder, nestling himself there as snugly as the cat had done.

"I like it here," Alphonse said decisively, as if there had ever been a question about it.

"It's home, then?"

"Definitely home."

A breeze rustled through, heralding a cooler night, and Alphonse steered them back towards the house. He paused just once, looking back for one last view of the garden before stepping over the threshold. A little potted plant sat inside the corner by the door, its sharp red leaves dark in the evening light, and tiny yellow flowers like sparks of magic. Its spice enveloped him like a blanket of cinnamon as he passed it, comforting now rather than overwhelming. Secure in Jacobi's arms, he followed the sounds of the girls' bright conversation into his new home.

ABOUT THE AUTHOR

Arden Powell is an author and illustrator from the Canadian East Coast. A nebulous entity, they live with a small terrier and an exorbitant number of houseplants, and have conversations with both. They write across multiple speculative fiction genres, and everything they write is queer.

Printed in Great Britain
by Amazon